DISNEY

FROZEN

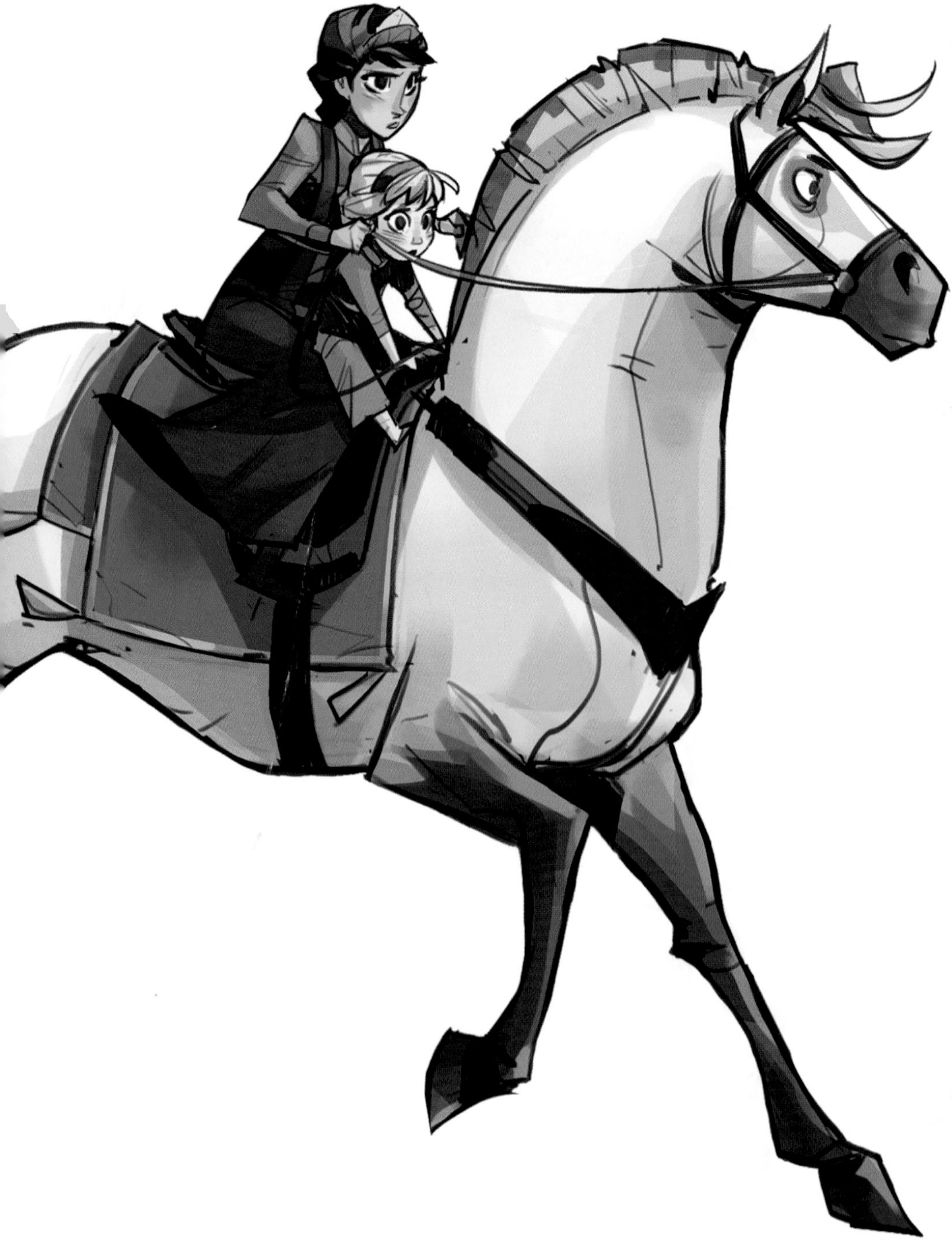

TRUE TREASURE

STORY & SCRIPT BY
JOE CARAMAGNA

LINE ART BY
KAWAII CREATIVE STUDIOS (PAGES 10–17, 20–26)
EDUARD PETROVICH (PAGES 7–9, 18–19, 28–39, 41–53, 56, 60, 65)
VERONICA DI LORENZO (PAGES 27, 40, 54–55, 57–59, 61–64, 66)

COLORING BY
KAWAII CREATIVE STUDIOS (PAGES 10–17, 20–26)
YANA CHINSTOVA AND **ANASTASIIA BELOUSOVA**
(PAGES 7–9, 18–19, 28–39, 41–53, 56, 60, 65)
WES DZIOBA (PAGES 27, 40, 54–55, 57–59, 61–64, 66)

LETTERING BY
RICHARD STARKINGS
& COMICRAFT'S JIMMY BETANCOURT

COVER ART BY
EDUARD PETROVICH

DARK HORSE BOOKS

DARK HORSE BOOKS

PRESIDENT AND PUBLISHER
MIKE RICHARDSON

EDITOR
FREDDYE MILLER

DESIGNER
BRENNAN THOME

ASSISTANT EDITOR
JUDY KHUU

DIGITAL ART TECHNICIAN
SAMANTHA HUMMER

Neil Hankerson Executive Vice President • **Tom Weddle** Chief Financial Officer • **Randy Stradley** Vice President of Publishing • **Nick McWhorter** Chief Business Development Officer • **Dale LaFountain** Chief Information Officer • **Matt Parkinson** Vice President of Marketing • **Cara Niece** Vice President of Production and Scheduling • **Mark Bernardi** Vice President of Book Trade and Digital Sales • **Ken Lizzi** General Counsel • **Dave Marshall** Editor in Chief • **Davey Estrada** Editorial Director • **Chris Warner** Senior Books Editor • **Cary Grazzini** Director of Specialty Projects • **Lia Ribacchi** Art Director • **Vanessa Todd-Holmes** Director of Print Purchasing • **Matt Dryer** Director of Digital Art and Prepress • **Michael Gombos** Senior Director of Licensed Publications • **Kari Yadro** Director of Custom Programs • **Kari Torson** Director of International Licensing • **Sean Brice** Director of Trade Sales

DISNEY PUBLISHING WORLDWIDE GLOBAL MAGAZINES, COMICS AND PARTWORKS

PUBLISHER Lynn Waggoner • EDITORIAL TEAM Bianca Coletti (Director, Magazines), Guido Frazzini (Director, Comics), Carlotta Quattrocolo (Executive Editor), Stefano Ambrosio (Executive Editor, New IP), Camilla Vedove (Senior Manager, Editorial Development), Behnoosh Khalili (Senior Editor), Julie Dorris (Senior Editor), Mina Riazi (Assistant Editor), Gabriela Capasso (Assistant Editor) • DESIGN Enrico Soave (Senior Designer) • ART Ken Shue (VP, Global Art), Manny Mederos (Senior Illustration Manager, Comics and Magazines), Roberto Santillo (Creative Director), Marco Ghiglione (Creative Manager), Stefano Attardi (Illustration Manager) • PORTFOLIO MANAGEMENT Olivia Ciancarelli (Director) • BUSINESS & MARKETING Mariantonietta Galla (Senior Manager, Franchise), Virpi Korhonen (Editorial Manager)

DISNEY FROZEN: TRUE TREASURE

Published by Dark Horse Books
A division of Dark Horse Comics LLC
10956 SE Main Street
Milwaukie, OR 97222

DarkHorse.com

To find a comics shop in your area, visit comicshoplocator.com

First edition: April 2020
ISBN 978-1-50671-705-0 | Digital ISBN 978-1-50671-706-7

1 3 5 7 9 10 8 6 4 2
Printed in China

WELCOME TO ARENDELLE!

ELSA

The queen of the kingdom of Arendelle and Anna's older sister. Elsa has the ability to create snow and ice. She is confident, composed, creative, and warmhearted.

ANNA

The princess of Arendelle and Elsa's younger sister. Anna has faith in others and puts a positive spin on every situation. She is compassionate, fearless, and doesn't shy away from following her heart—no matter what.

OLAF

A snowman that Elsa brought to life. Olaf is a friend to all! He likes warm hugs and he is full of wonder and optimism—nothing can bring him down.

KRISTOFF

An ice harvester and the official ice master and deliverer of Arendelle. Raised by trolls in the mountains, he understands the importance of friends, family, and being true to yourself. He lives with his reindeer Sven.

SVEN

A reindeer and loyal best friend to Kristoff. They have regular conversations, and though Sven cannot communicate in words, sometimes Kristoff speaks for him. He enjoys carrots and lichen.

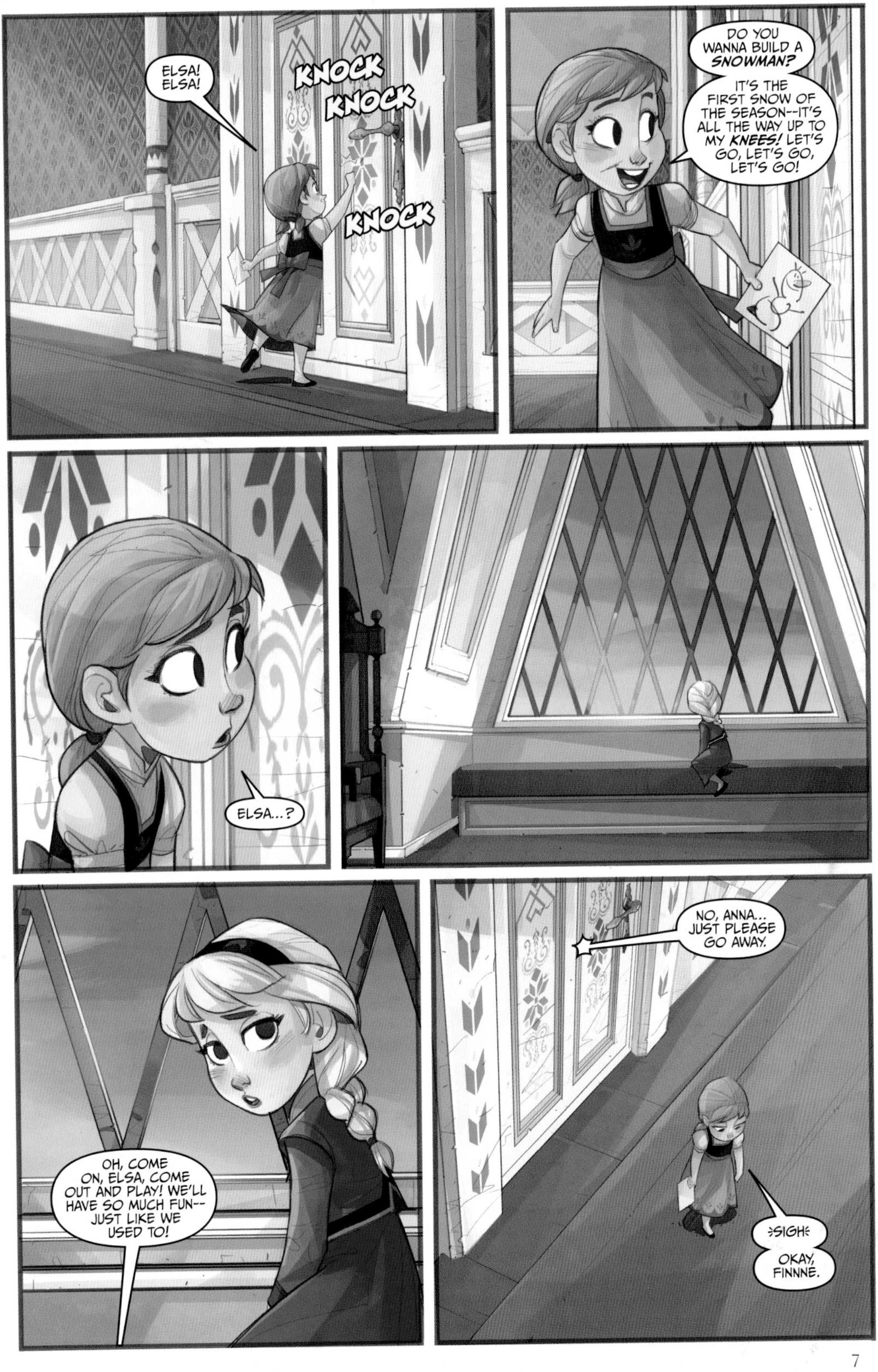
ELSA! ELSA!
KNOCK
KNOCK
KNOCK
DO YOU WANNA BUILD A SNOWMAN?
IT'S THE FIRST SNOW OF THE SEASON--IT'S ALL THE WAY UP TO MY KNEES! LET'S GO, LET'S GO, LET'S GO!
ELSA...?
OH, COME ON, ELSA, COME OUT AND PLAY! WE'LL HAVE SO MUCH FUN--JUST LIKE WE USED TO!
NO, ANNA... JUST PLEASE GO AWAY.
SIGH
OKAY, FINNNE.

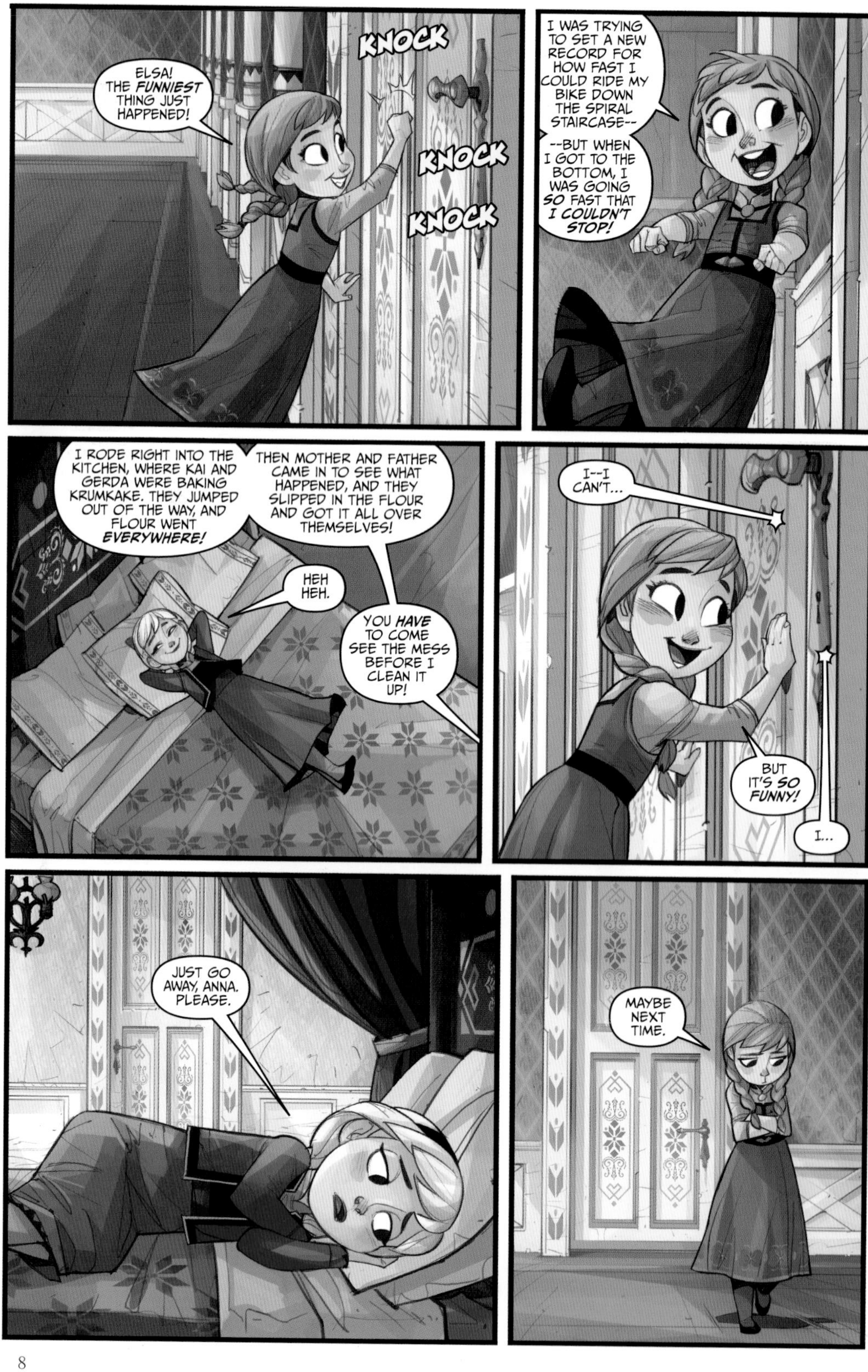
KNOCK
ELSA! THE FUNNIEST THING JUST HAPPENED!
KNOCK
KNOCK
I WAS TRYING TO SET A NEW RECORD FOR HOW FAST I COULD RIDE MY BIKE DOWN THE SPIRAL STAIRCASE--
--BUT WHEN I GOT TO THE BOTTOM, I WAS GOING SO FAST THAT I COULDN'T STOP!
I RODE RIGHT INTO THE KITCHEN, WHERE KAI AND GERDA WERE BAKING KRUMKAKE. THEY JUMPED OUT OF THE WAY, AND FLOUR WENT EVERYWHERE!
THEN MOTHER AND FATHER CAME IN TO SEE WHAT HAPPENED, AND THEY SLIPPED IN THE FLOUR AND GOT IT ALL OVER THEMSELVES!
HEH HEH.
YOU HAVE TO COME SEE THE MESS BEFORE I CLEAN IT UP!
I--I CAN'T...
BUT IT'S SO FUNNY!
I...
JUST GO AWAY, ANNA. PLEASE.
MAYBE NEXT TIME.

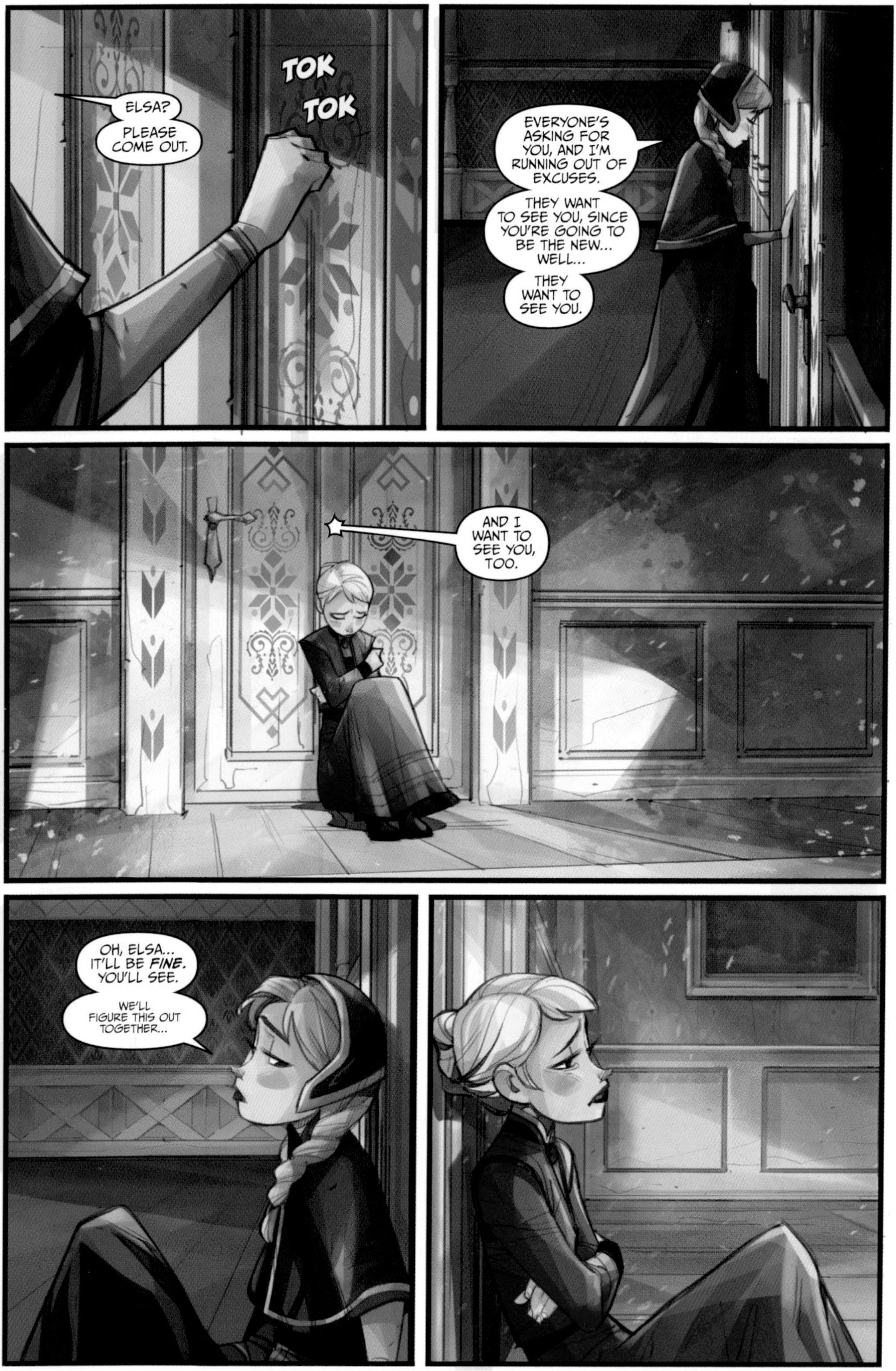
TOK
TOK
ELSA? PLEASE COME OUT.
EVERYONE'S ASKING FOR YOU, AND I'M RUNNING OUT OF EXCUSES.
THEY WANT TO SEE YOU, SINCE YOU'RE GOING TO BE THE NEW... WELL...
THEY WANT TO SEE YOU.
AND I WANT TO SEE YOU, TOO.
OH, ELSA... IT'LL BE *FINE.* YOU'LL SEE.
WE'LL FIGURE THIS OUT TOGETHER...

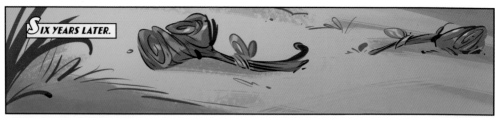

THE MEMORIAL SITE OF KING AGNARR AND QUEEN IDUNA.

WHO ARE THEY, MAMA?

THAT WAS KING AGNARR AND QUEEN IDUNA--QUEEN ELSA AND PRINCESS ANNA'S MOTHER AND FATHER.

WHAT HAPPENED TO THEM?

THEY... WELL, THEY...

OH-- QUEEN ELSA AND PRINCESS ANNA HAVE ARRIVED.

READY, ELSA?

HEY, ARE... ARE YOU OKAY?

OF COURSE.

THERE ARE SO MANY PEOPLE...

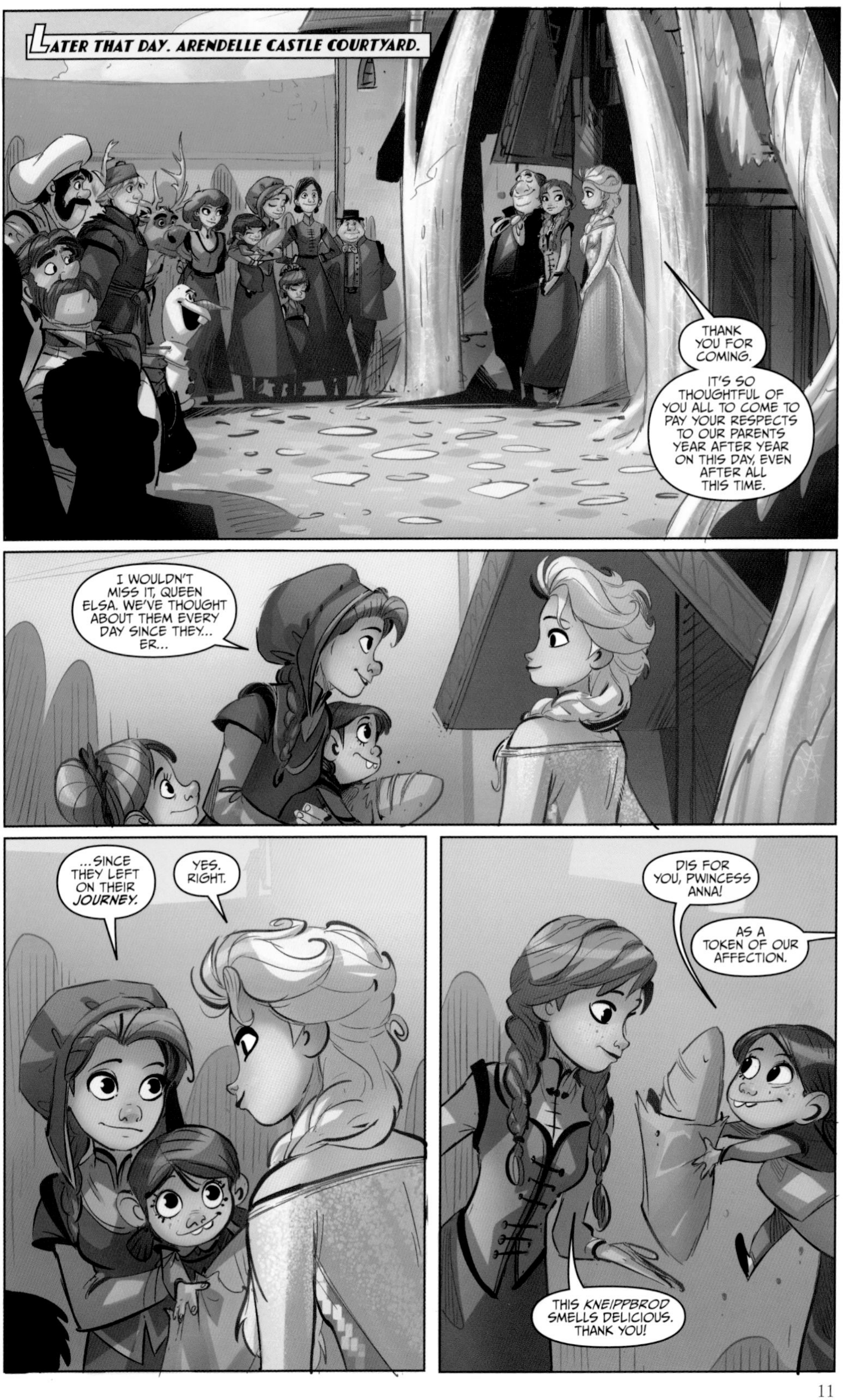
LATER THAT DAY. ARENDELLE CASTLE COURTYARD.
THANK YOU FOR COMING.
IT'S SO THOUGHTFUL OF YOU ALL TO COME TO PAY YOUR RESPECTS TO OUR PARENTS YEAR AFTER YEAR ON THIS DAY, EVEN AFTER ALL THIS TIME.
I WOULDN'T MISS IT, QUEEN ELSA. WE'VE THOUGHT ABOUT THEM EVERY DAY SINCE THEY... ER...
...SINCE THEY LEFT ON THEIR *JOURNEY.*
YES. RIGHT.
DIS FOR YOU, PWINCESS ANNA!
AS A TOKEN OF OUR AFFECTION.
THIS *KNEIPPBROD* SMELLS DELICIOUS. THANK YOU!

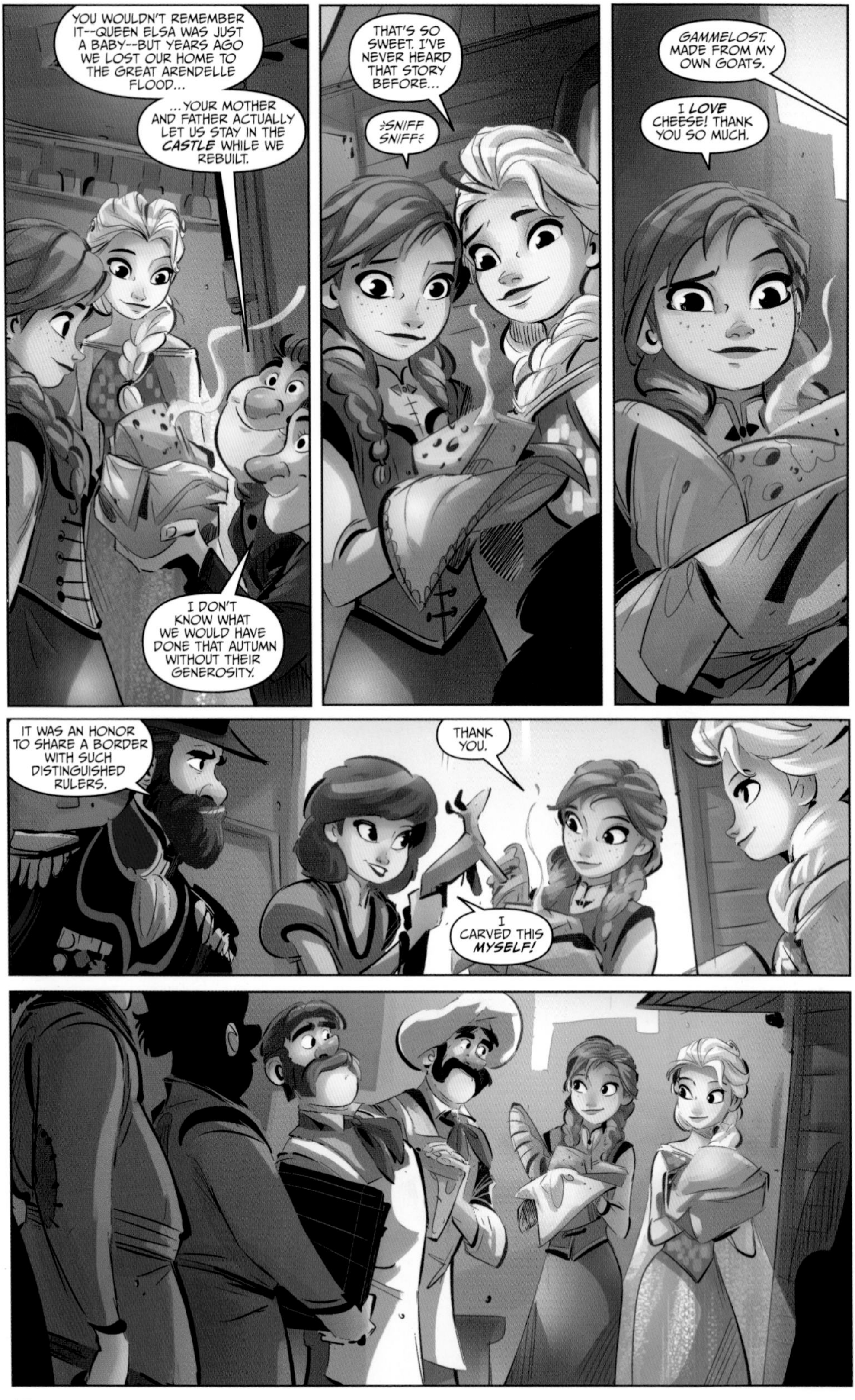
YOU WOULDN'T REMEMBER IT--QUEEN ELSA WAS JUST A BABY--BUT YEARS AGO WE LOST OUR HOME TO THE GREAT ARENDELLE FLOOD...
...YOUR MOTHER AND FATHER ACTUALLY LET US STAY IN THE CASTLE WHILE WE REBUILT.
I DON'T KNOW WHAT WE WOULD HAVE DONE THAT AUTUMN WITHOUT THEIR GENEROSITY.
THAT'S SO SWEET. I'VE NEVER HEARD THAT STORY BEFORE...
SNIFF SNIFF
GAMMELOST. MADE FROM MY OWN GOATS.
I LOVE CHEESE! THANK YOU SO MUCH.
IT WAS AN HONOR TO SHARE A BORDER WITH SUCH DISTINGUISHED RULERS.
THANK YOU.
I CARVED THIS MYSELF!

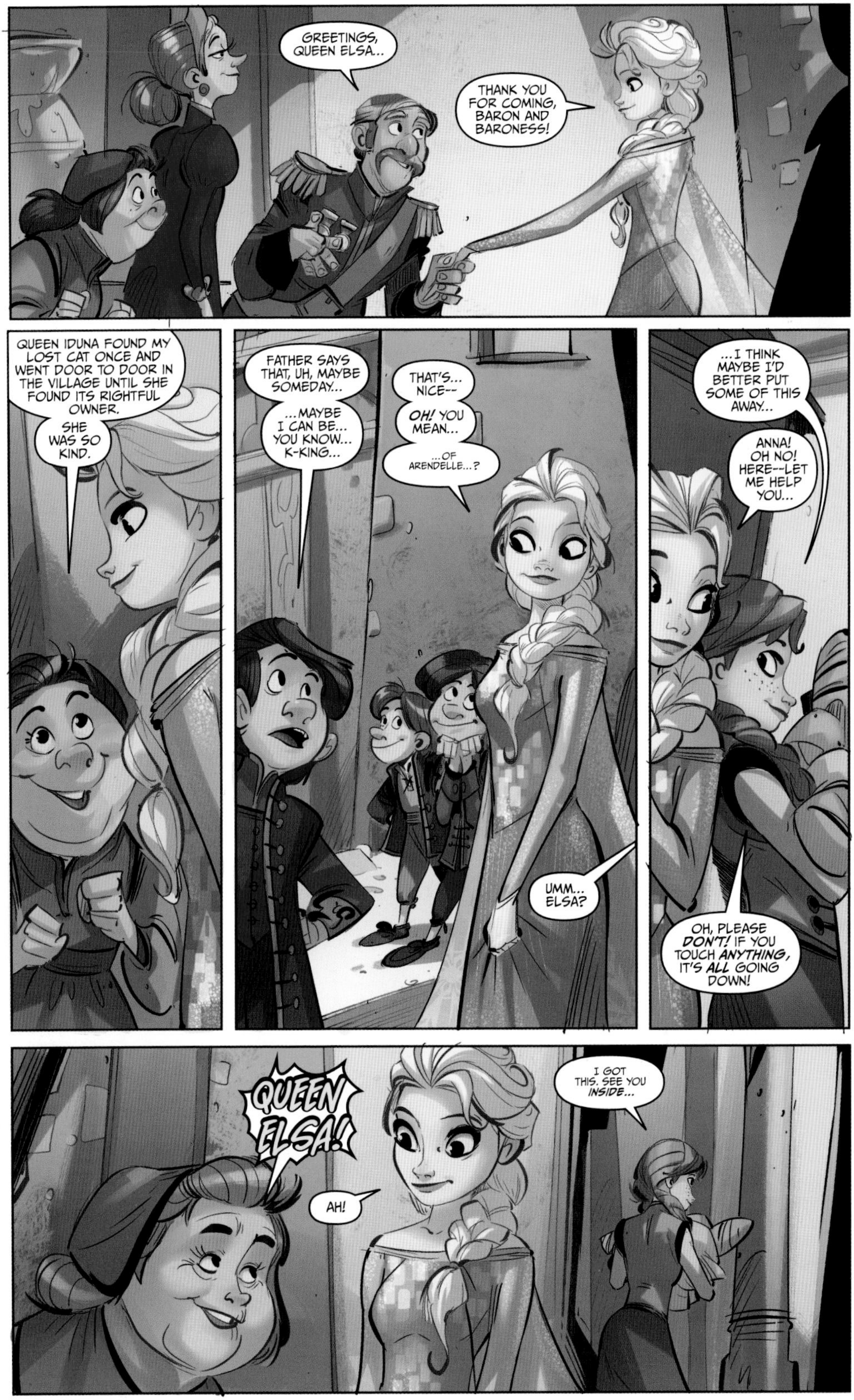
GREETINGS, QUEEN ELSA...
THANK YOU FOR COMING, BARON AND BARONESS!
QUEEN IDUNA FOUND MY LOST CAT ONCE AND WENT DOOR TO DOOR IN THE VILLAGE UNTIL SHE FOUND ITS RIGHTFUL OWNER.
SHE WAS SO KIND.
FATHER SAYS THAT, UH, MAYBE SOMEDAY...
...MAYBE I CAN BE... YOU KNOW... K-KING...
THAT'S... NICE--
OH! YOU MEAN...
...OF ARENDELLE...?
UMM... ELSA?
...I THINK MAYBE I'D BETTER PUT SOME OF THIS AWAY...
ANNA! OH NO! HERE--LET ME HELP YOU...
OH, PLEASE DON'T! IF YOU TOUCH ANYTHING, IT'S ALL GOING DOWN!
QUEEN ELSA!
AH!
I GOT THIS. SEE YOU INSIDE...

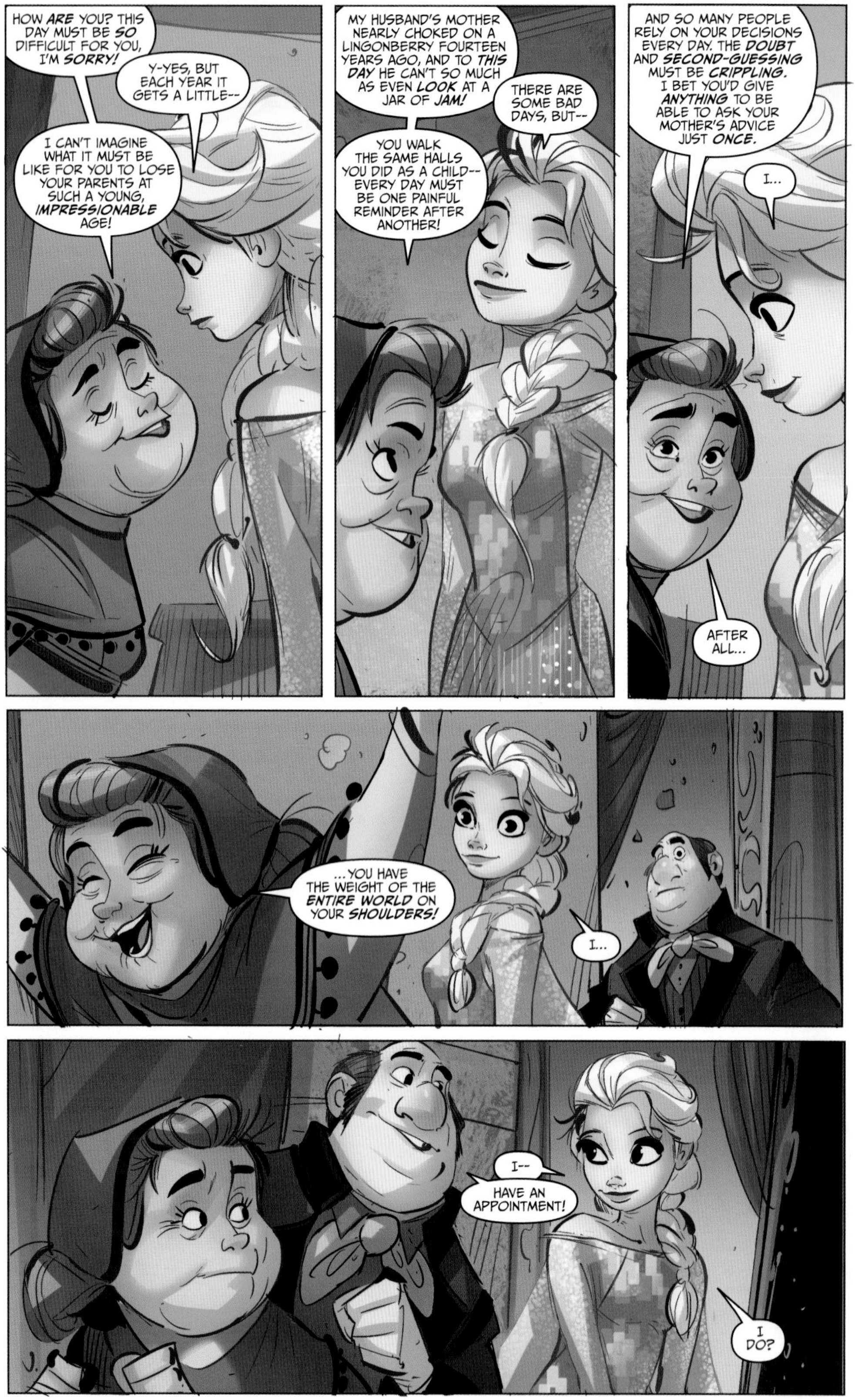
HOW ARE YOU? THIS DAY MUST BE SO DIFFICULT FOR YOU, I'M SORRY!
Y-YES, BUT EACH YEAR IT GETS A LITTLE--
I CAN'T IMAGINE WHAT IT MUST BE LIKE FOR YOU TO LOSE YOUR PARENTS AT SUCH A YOUNG, IMPRESSIONABLE AGE!
MY HUSBAND'S MOTHER NEARLY CHOKED ON A LINGONBERRY FOURTEEN YEARS AGO, AND TO THIS DAY HE CAN'T SO MUCH AS EVEN LOOK AT A JAR OF JAM!
THERE ARE SOME BAD DAYS, BUT--
YOU WALK THE SAME HALLS YOU DID AS A CHILD-- EVERY DAY MUST BE ONE PAINFUL REMINDER AFTER ANOTHER!
AND SO MANY PEOPLE RELY ON YOUR DECISIONS EVERY DAY. THE DOUBT AND SECOND-GUESSING MUST BE CRIPPLING. I BET YOU'D GIVE ANYTHING TO BE ABLE TO ASK YOUR MOTHER'S ADVICE JUST ONCE.
I...
AFTER ALL...
...YOU HAVE THE WEIGHT OF THE ENTIRE WORLD ON YOUR SHOULDERS!
I...
I--
HAVE AN APPOINTMENT!
I DO?

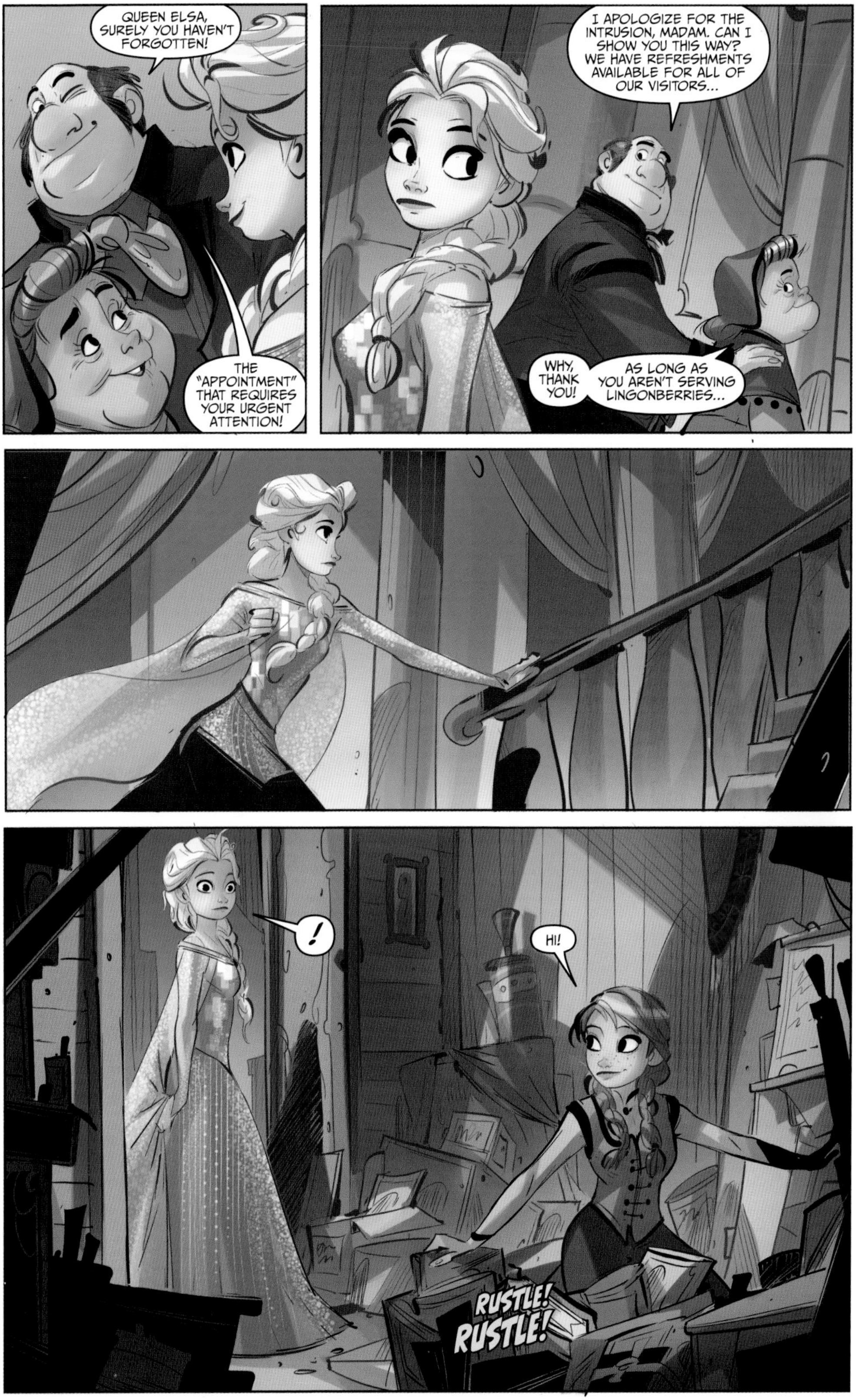
QUEEN ELSA, SURELY YOU HAVEN'T FORGOTTEN!
THE "APPOINTMENT" THAT REQUIRES YOUR URGENT ATTENTION!
I APOLOGIZE FOR THE INTRUSION, MADAM. CAN I SHOW YOU THIS WAY? WE HAVE REFRESHMENTS AVAILABLE FOR ALL OF OUR VISITORS...
WHY, THANK YOU!
AS LONG AS YOU AREN'T SERVING LINGONBERRIES...
!
HI!
RUSTLE! RUSTLE!

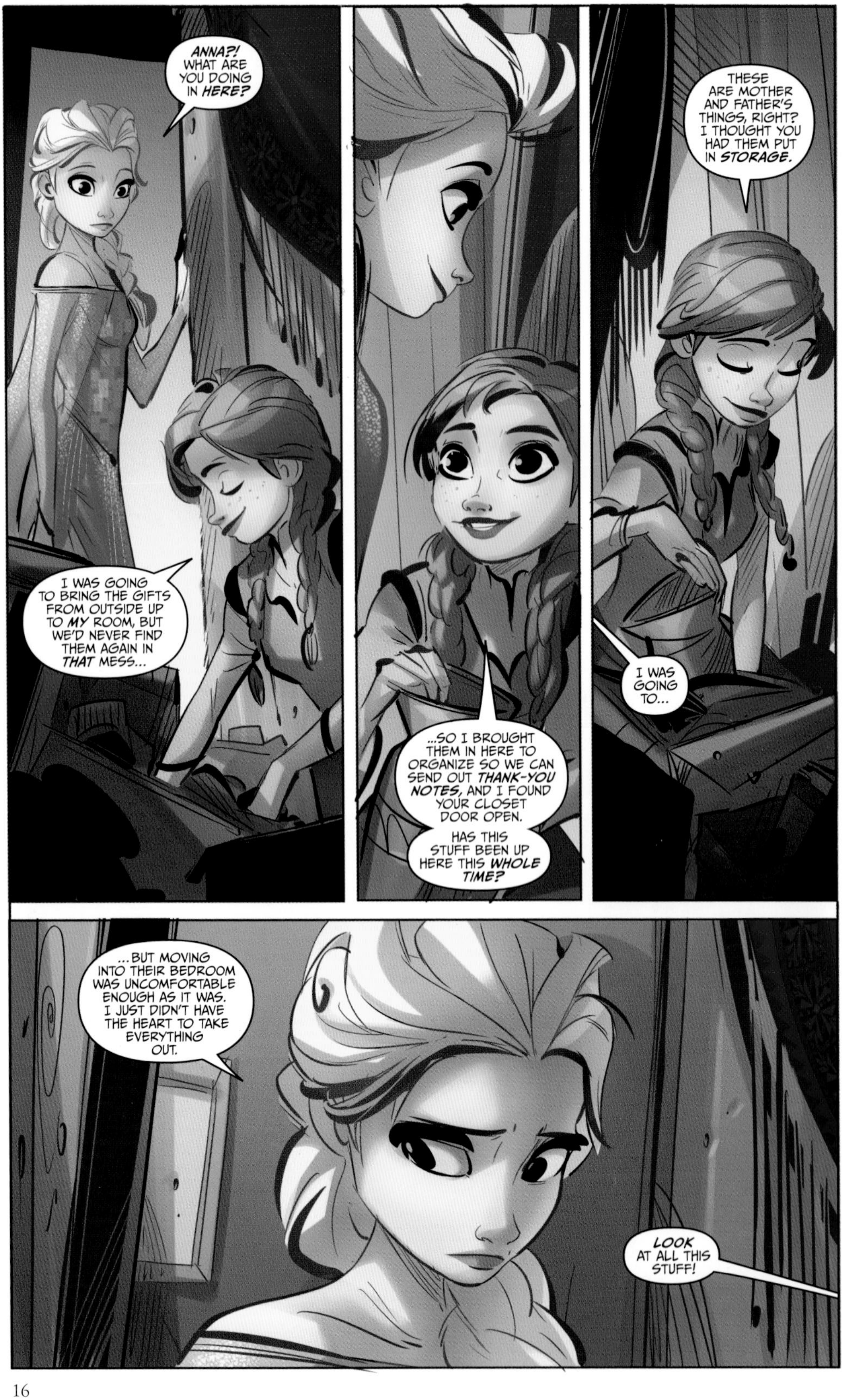

ANNA?! WHAT ARE YOU DOING IN HERE?
I WAS GOING TO BRING THE GIFTS FROM OUTSIDE UP TO MY ROOM, BUT WE'D NEVER FIND THEM AGAIN IN THAT MESS...
...SO I BROUGHT THEM IN HERE TO ORGANIZE SO WE CAN SEND OUT THANK-YOU NOTES, AND I FOUND YOUR CLOSET DOOR OPEN.
HAS THIS STUFF BEEN UP HERE THIS WHOLE TIME?
THESE ARE MOTHER AND FATHER'S THINGS, RIGHT? I THOUGHT YOU HAD THEM PUT IN STORAGE.
I WAS GOING TO...
...BUT MOVING INTO THEIR BEDROOM WAS UNCOMFORTABLE ENOUGH AS IT WAS. I JUST DIDN'T HAVE THE HEART TO TAKE EVERYTHING OUT.
LOOK AT ALL THIS STUFF!

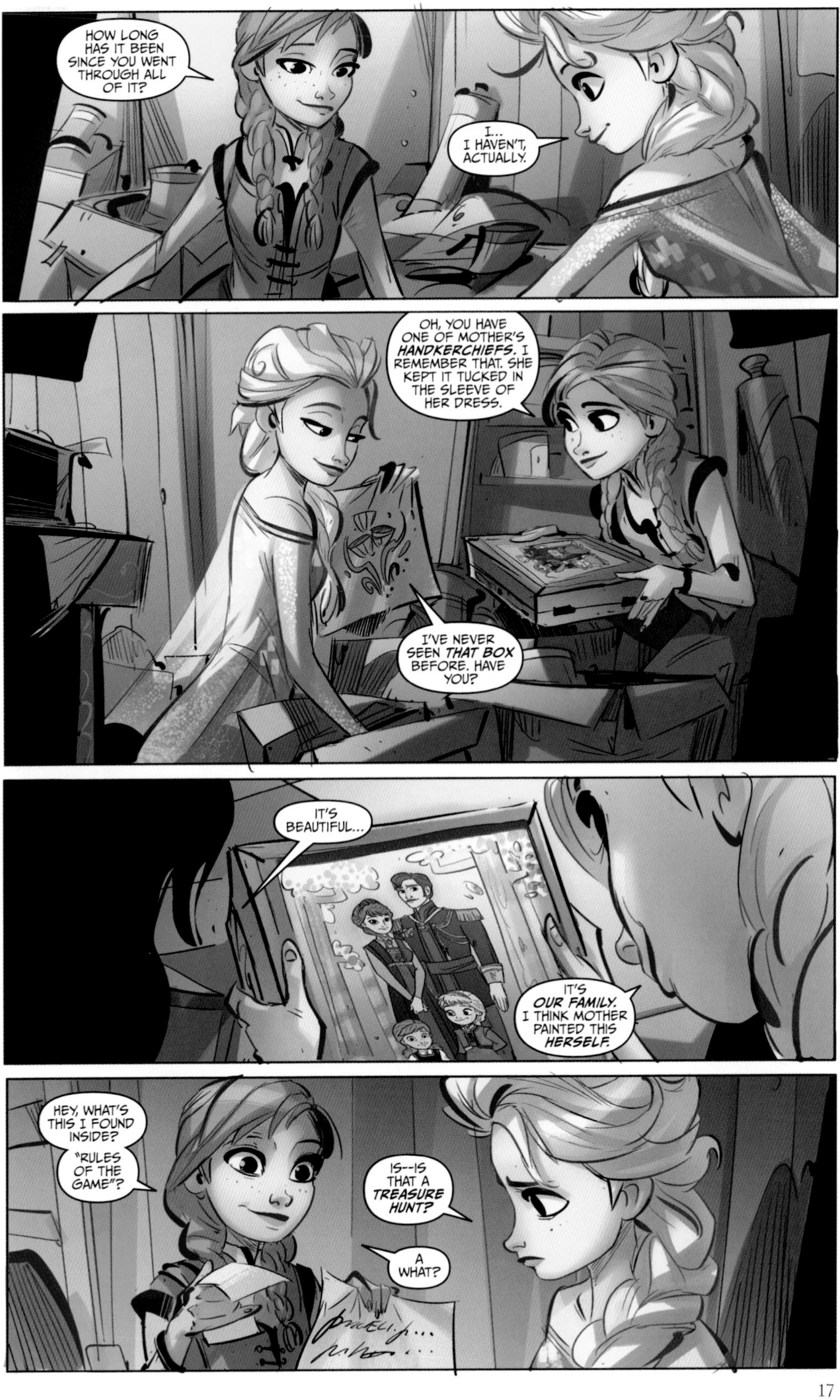
HOW LONG HAS IT BEEN SINCE YOU WENT THROUGH ALL OF IT?
I... I HAVEN'T, ACTUALLY.
OH, YOU HAVE ONE OF MOTHER'S **HANDKERCHIEFS.** I REMEMBER THAT. SHE KEPT IT TUCKED IN THE SLEEVE OF HER DRESS.
I'VE NEVER SEEN ***THAT BOX*** BEFORE. HAVE YOU?
IT'S BEAUTIFUL...
IT'S ***OUR FAMILY.*** I THINK MOTHER PAINTED THIS ***HERSELF.***
HEY, WHAT'S THIS I FOUND INSIDE? "RULES OF THE GAME"?
IS--IS THAT A ***TREASURE HUNT?***
A WHAT?

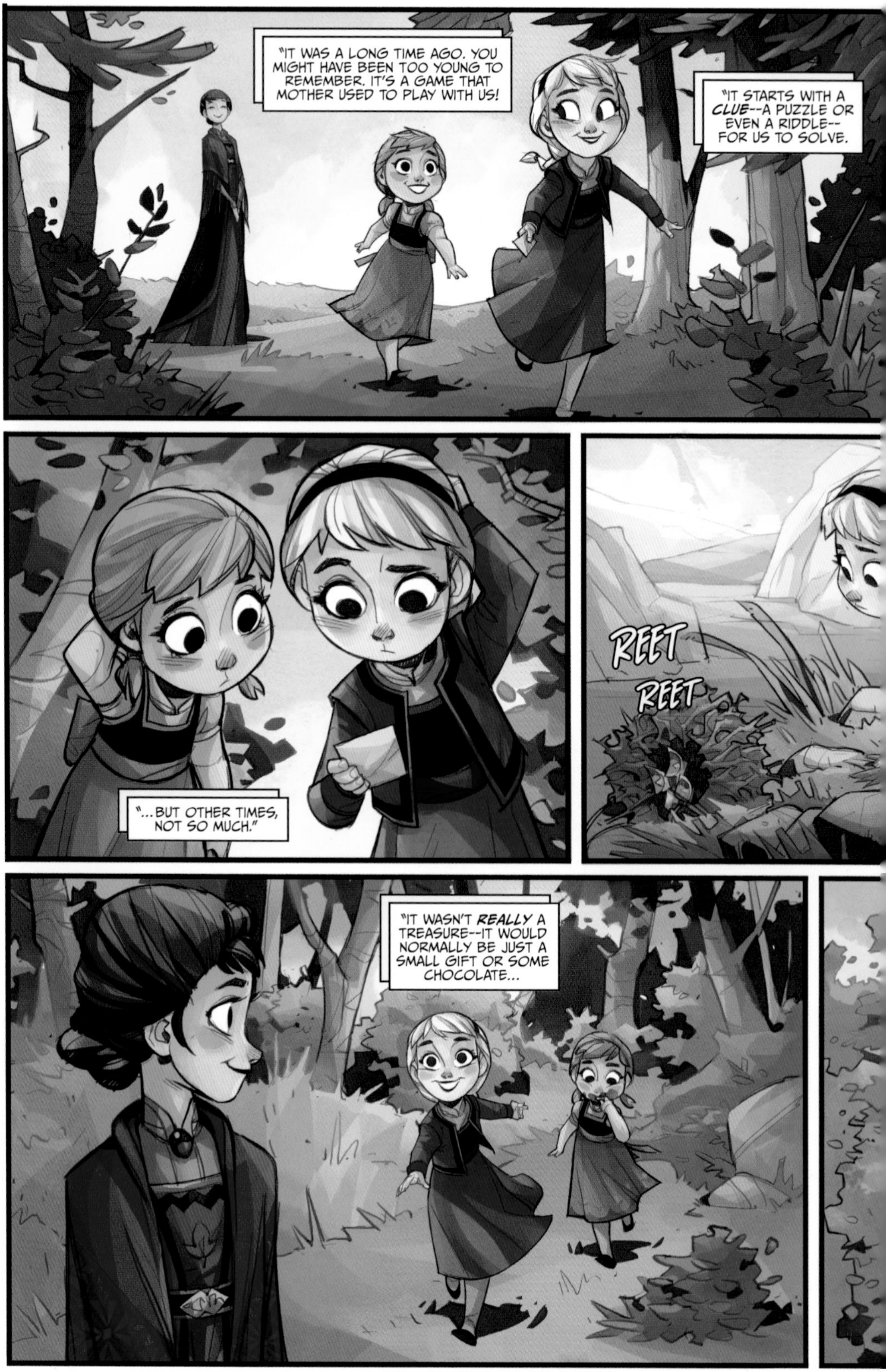
"IT WAS A LONG TIME AGO. YOU MIGHT HAVE BEEN TOO YOUNG TO REMEMBER. IT'S A GAME THAT MOTHER USED TO PLAY WITH US!
"IT STARTS WITH A *CLUE*--A PUZZLE OR EVEN A RIDDLE--FOR US TO SOLVE.
"...BUT OTHER TIMES, NOT SO MUCH."
REET
REET
"IT WASN'T *REALLY* A TREASURE--IT WOULD NORMALLY BE JUST A SMALL GIFT OR SOME CHOCOLATE...

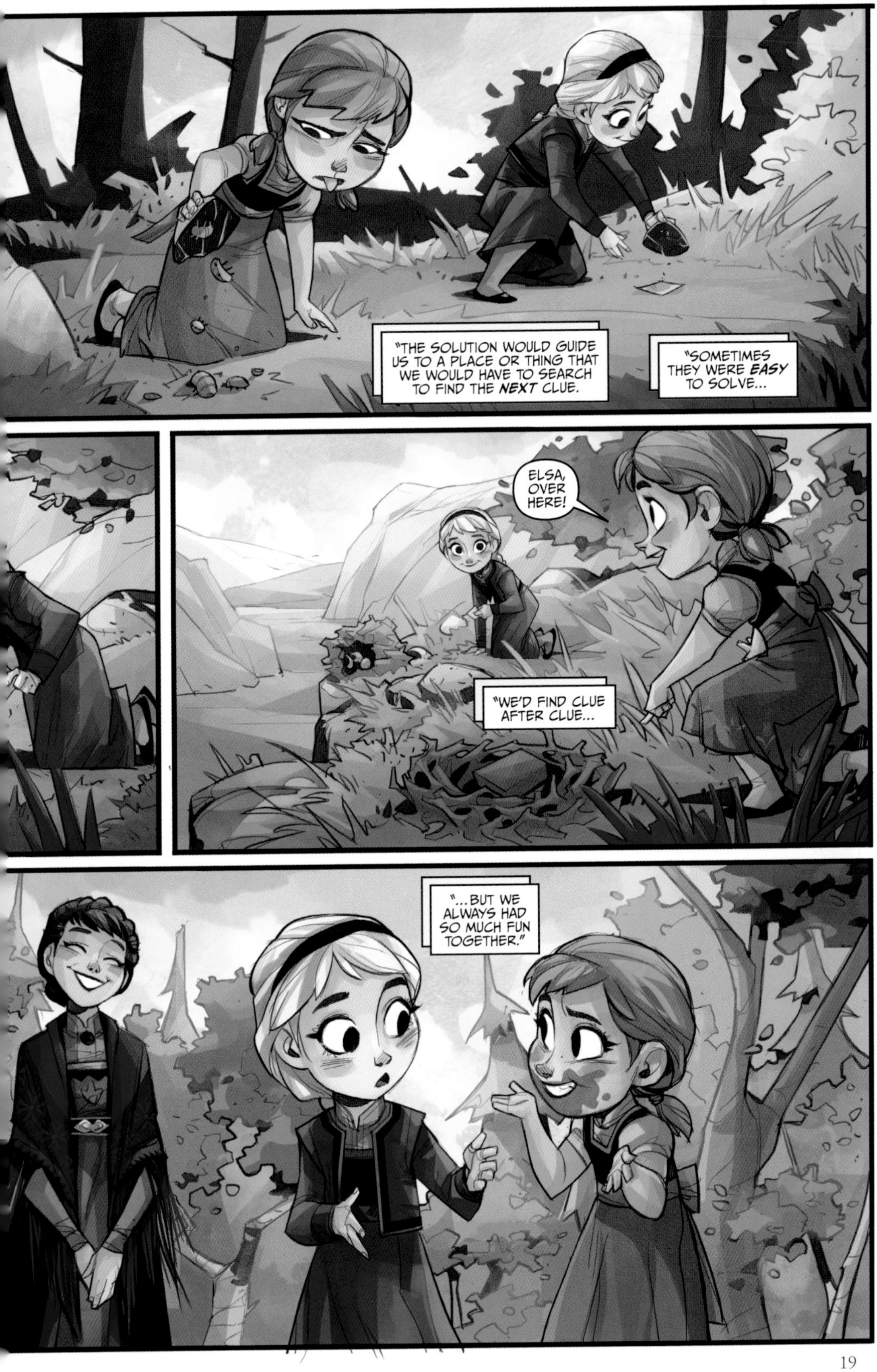
"THE SOLUTION WOULD GUIDE US TO A PLACE OR THING THAT WE WOULD HAVE TO SEARCH TO FIND THE NEXT CLUE.
"SOMETIMES THEY WERE EASY TO SOLVE...
ELSA, OVER HERE!
"WE'D FIND CLUE AFTER CLUE...
"...BUT WE ALWAYS HAD SO MUCH FUN TOGETHER."

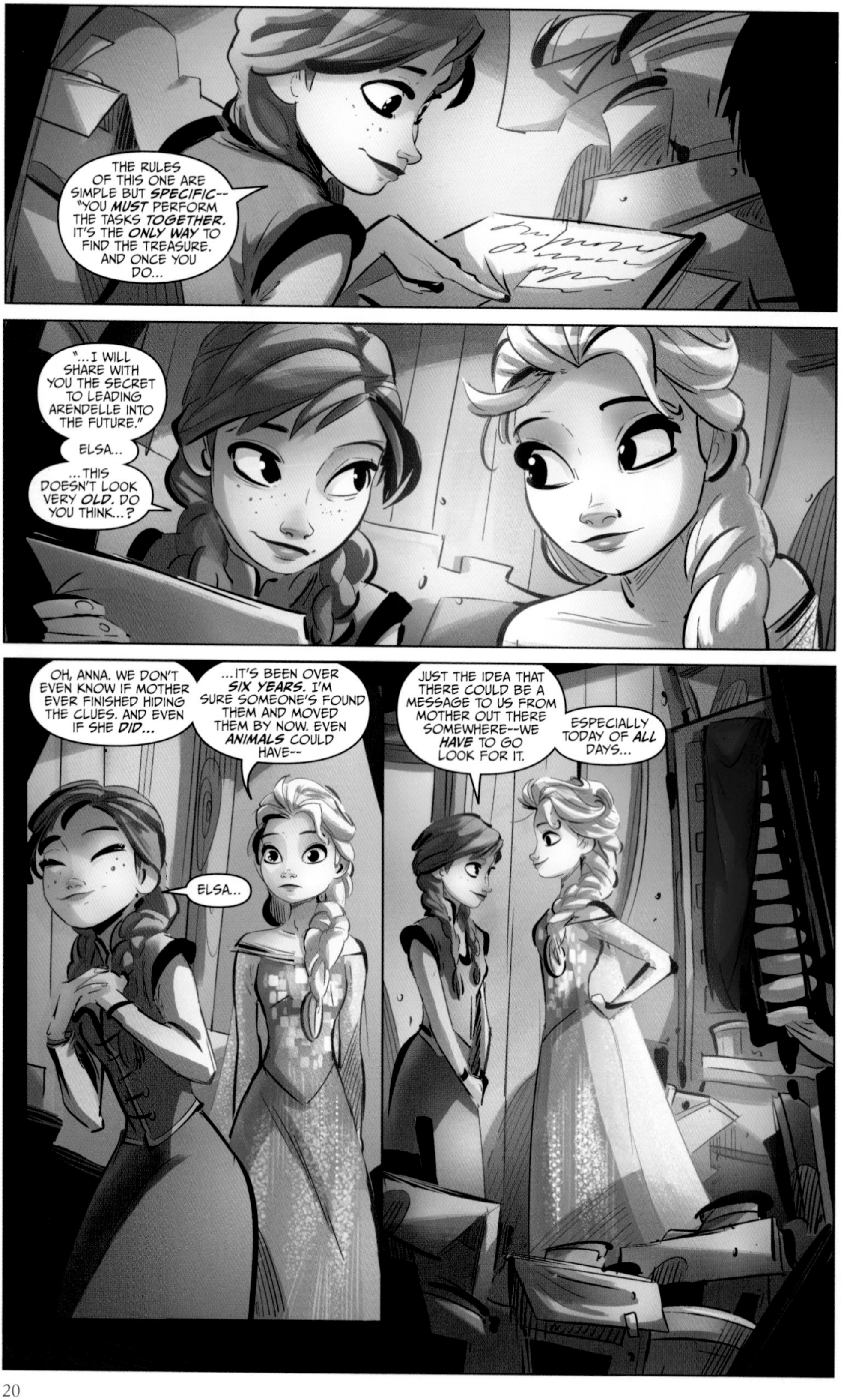
THE RULES OF THIS ONE ARE SIMPLE BUT SPECIFIC-- "YOU MUST PERFORM THE TASKS TOGETHER. IT'S THE ONLY WAY TO FIND THE TREASURE. AND ONCE YOU DO...
"...I WILL SHARE WITH YOU THE SECRET TO LEADING ARENDELLE INTO THE FUTURE."
ELSA...
...THIS DOESN'T LOOK VERY OLD. DO YOU THINK...?
OH, ANNA. WE DON'T EVEN KNOW IF MOTHER EVER FINISHED HIDING THE CLUES. AND EVEN IF SHE DID...
...IT'S BEEN OVER SIX YEARS. I'M SURE SOMEONE'S FOUND THEM AND MOVED THEM BY NOW. EVEN ANIMALS COULD HAVE--
ELSA...
JUST THE IDEA THAT THERE COULD BE A MESSAGE TO US FROM MOTHER OUT THERE SOMEWHERE--WE HAVE TO GO LOOK FOR IT.
ESPECIALLY TODAY OF ALL DAYS...

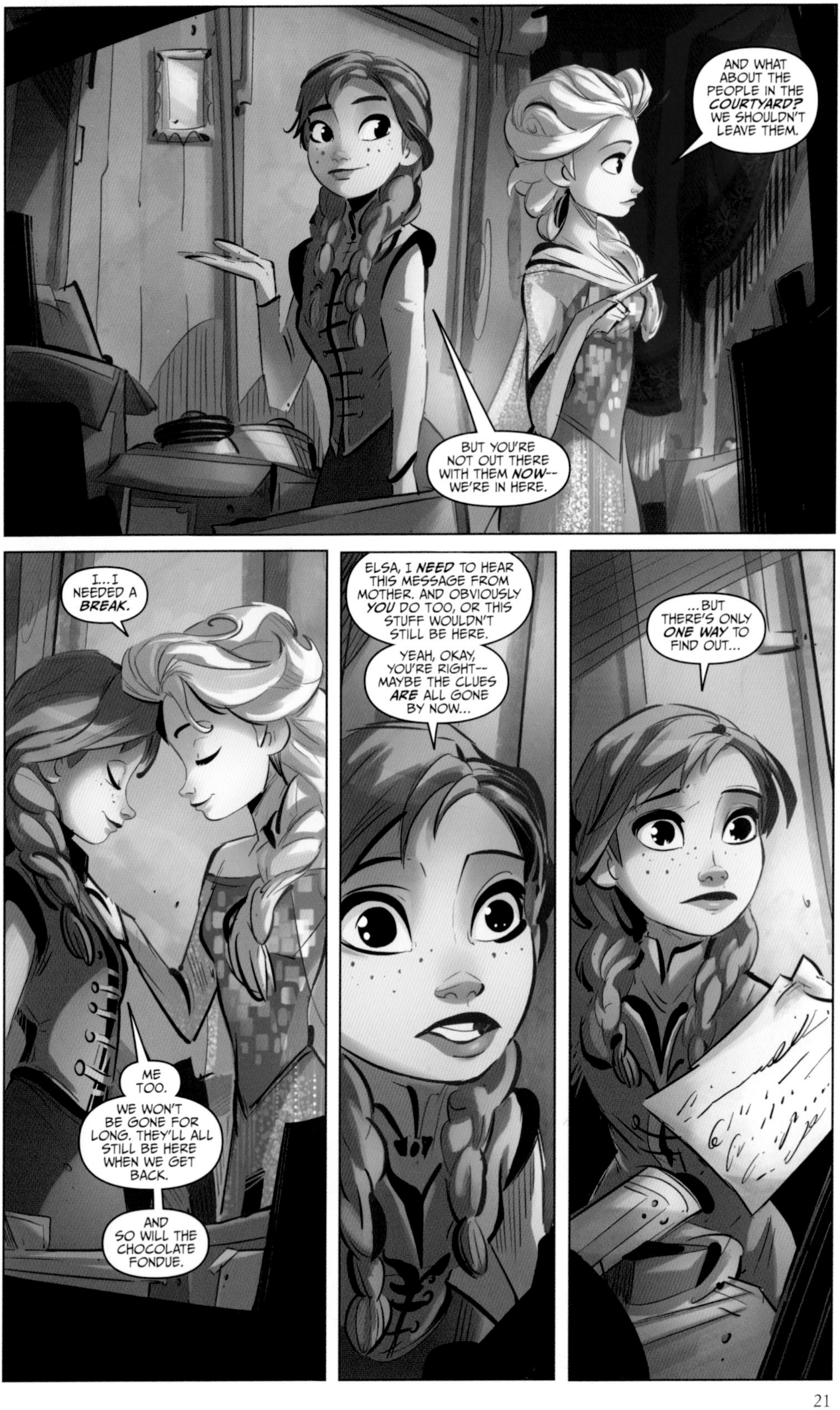
AND WHAT ABOUT THE PEOPLE IN THE COURTYARD? WE SHOULDN'T LEAVE THEM.
BUT YOU'RE NOT OUT THERE WITH THEM NOW-- WE'RE IN HERE.
I...I NEEDED A BREAK.
ME TOO.
WE WON'T BE GONE FOR LONG. THEY'LL ALL STILL BE HERE WHEN WE GET BACK.
AND SO WILL THE CHOCOLATE FONDUE.
ELSA, I NEED TO HEAR THIS MESSAGE FROM MOTHER. AND OBVIOUSLY YOU DO TOO, OR THIS STUFF WOULDN'T STILL BE HERE.
YEAH, OKAY, YOU'RE RIGHT-- MAYBE THE CLUES ARE ALL GONE BY NOW...
...BUT THERE'S ONLY ONE WAY TO FIND OUT...

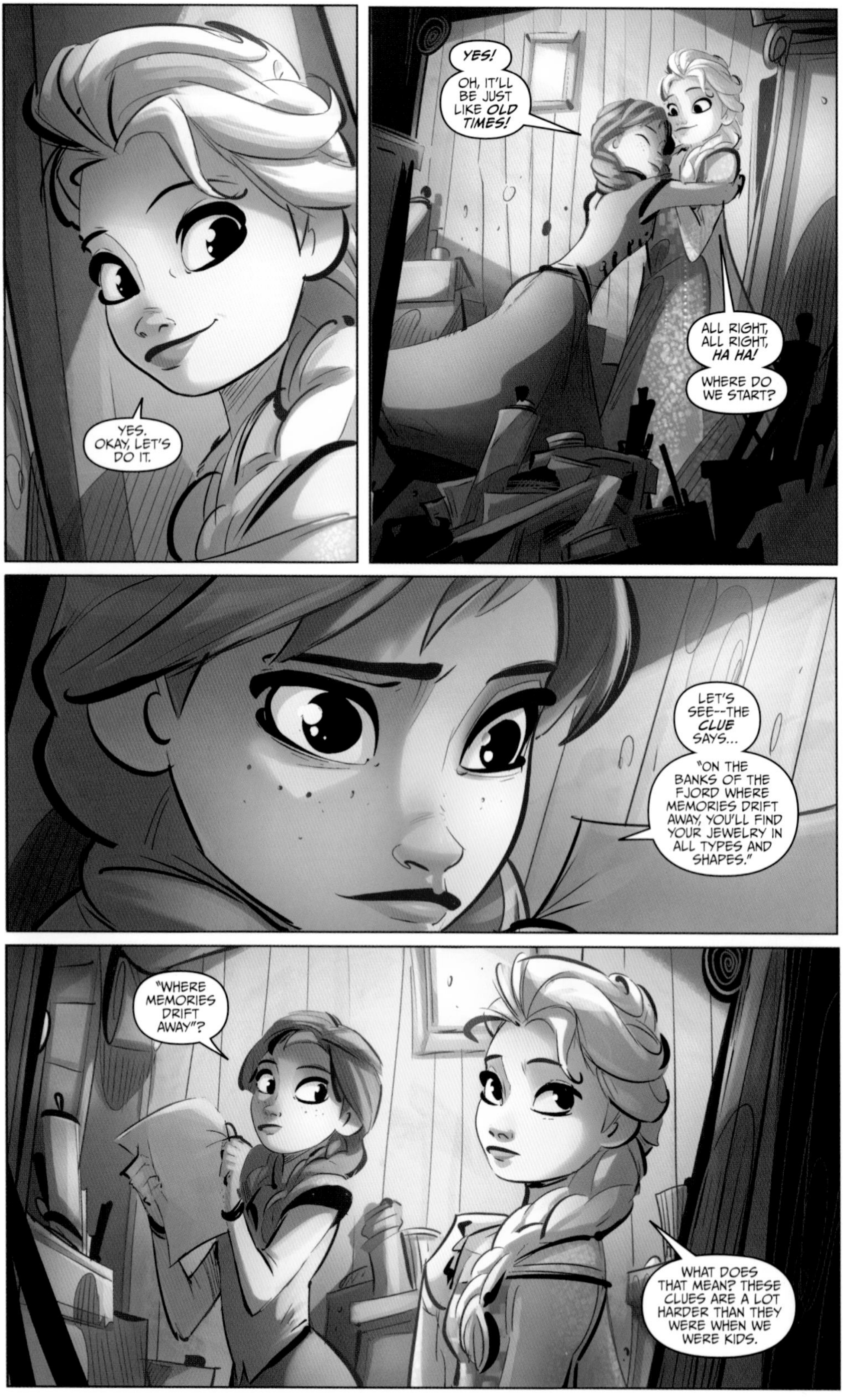
YES. OKAY, LET'S DO IT.
YES!
OH, IT'LL BE JUST LIKE OLD TIMES!
ALL RIGHT, ALL RIGHT, HA HA!
WHERE DO WE START?
LET'S SEE--THE CLUE SAYS...
"ON THE BANKS OF THE FJORD WHERE MEMORIES DRIFT AWAY, YOU'LL FIND YOUR JEWELRY IN ALL TYPES AND SHAPES."
"WHERE MEMORIES DRIFT AWAY"?
WHAT DOES THAT MEAN? THESE CLUES ARE A LOT HARDER THAN THEY WERE WHEN WE WERE KIDS.

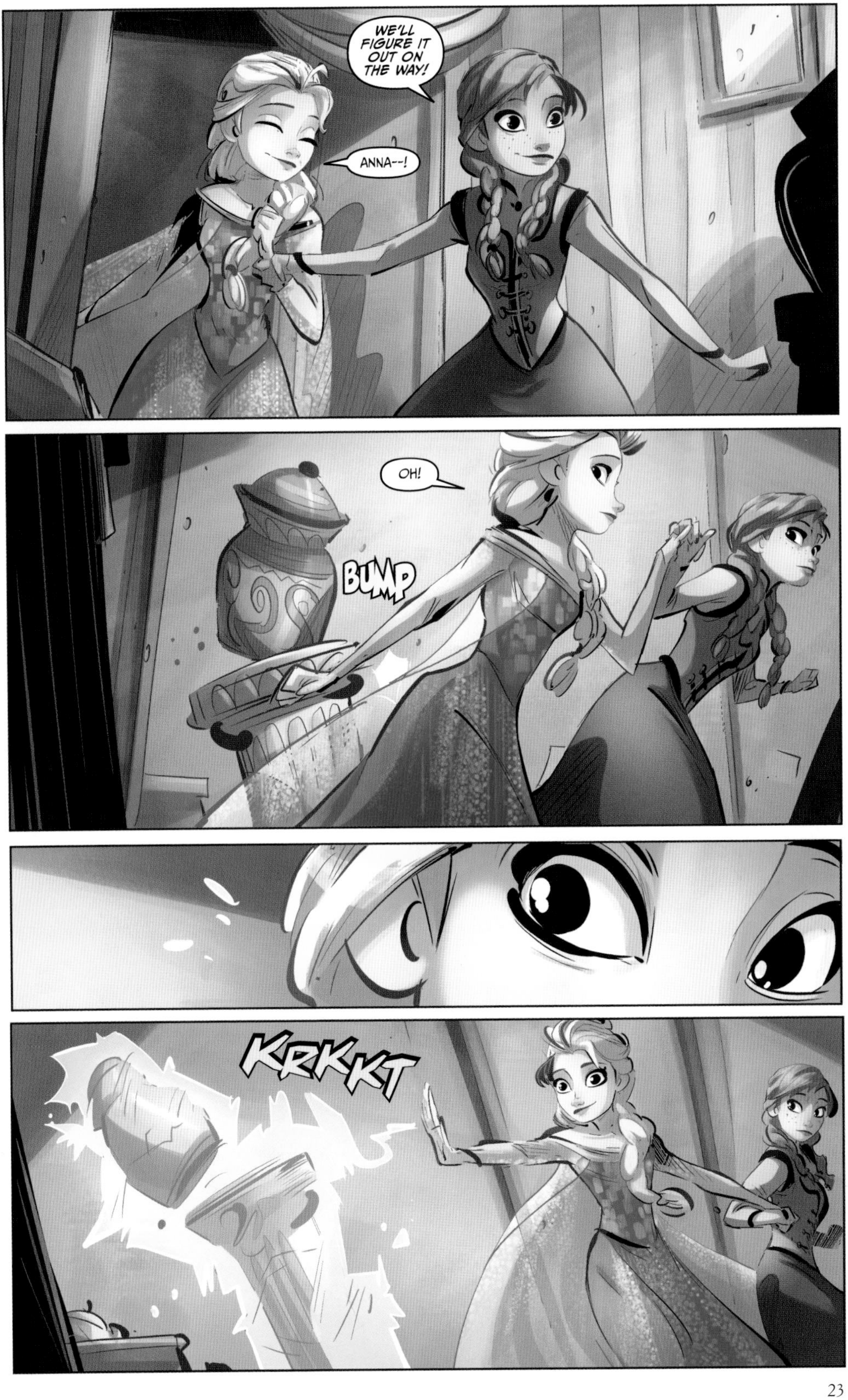
WE'LL FIGURE IT OUT ON THE WAY!
ANNA--!
OH!
BUMP
KRKKT

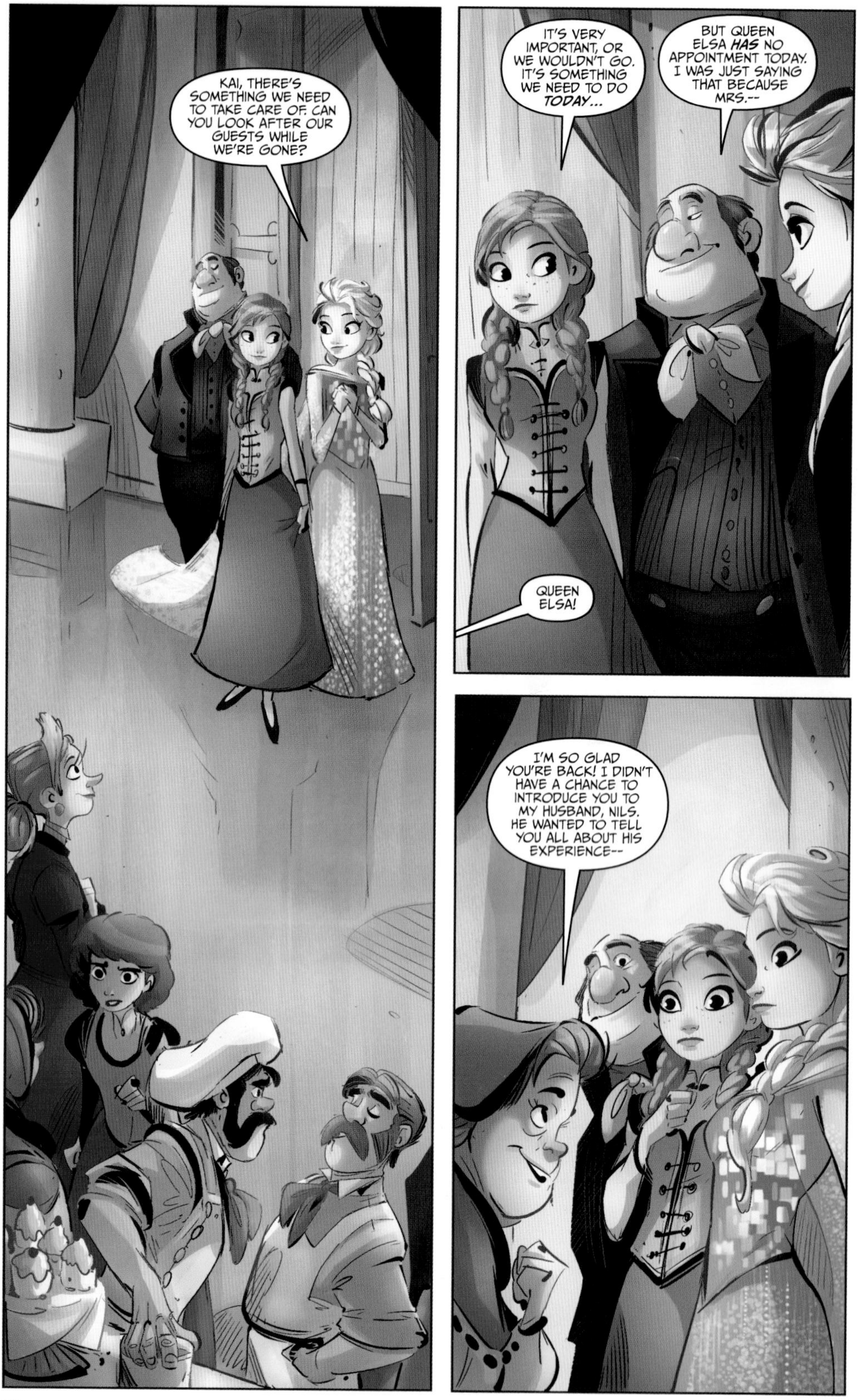
KAI, THERE'S SOMETHING WE NEED TO TAKE CARE OF. CAN YOU LOOK AFTER OUR GUESTS WHILE WE'RE GONE?
BUT QUEEN ELSA *HAS* NO APPOINTMENT TODAY. I WAS JUST SAYING THAT BECAUSE MRS.--
IT'S VERY IMPORTANT, OR WE WOULDN'T GO. IT'S SOMETHING WE NEED TO DO *TODAY*...
QUEEN ELSA!
I'M SO GLAD YOU'RE BACK! I DIDN'T HAVE A CHANCE TO INTRODUCE YOU TO MY HUSBAND, NILS. HE WANTED TO TELL YOU ALL ABOUT HIS EXPERIENCE--

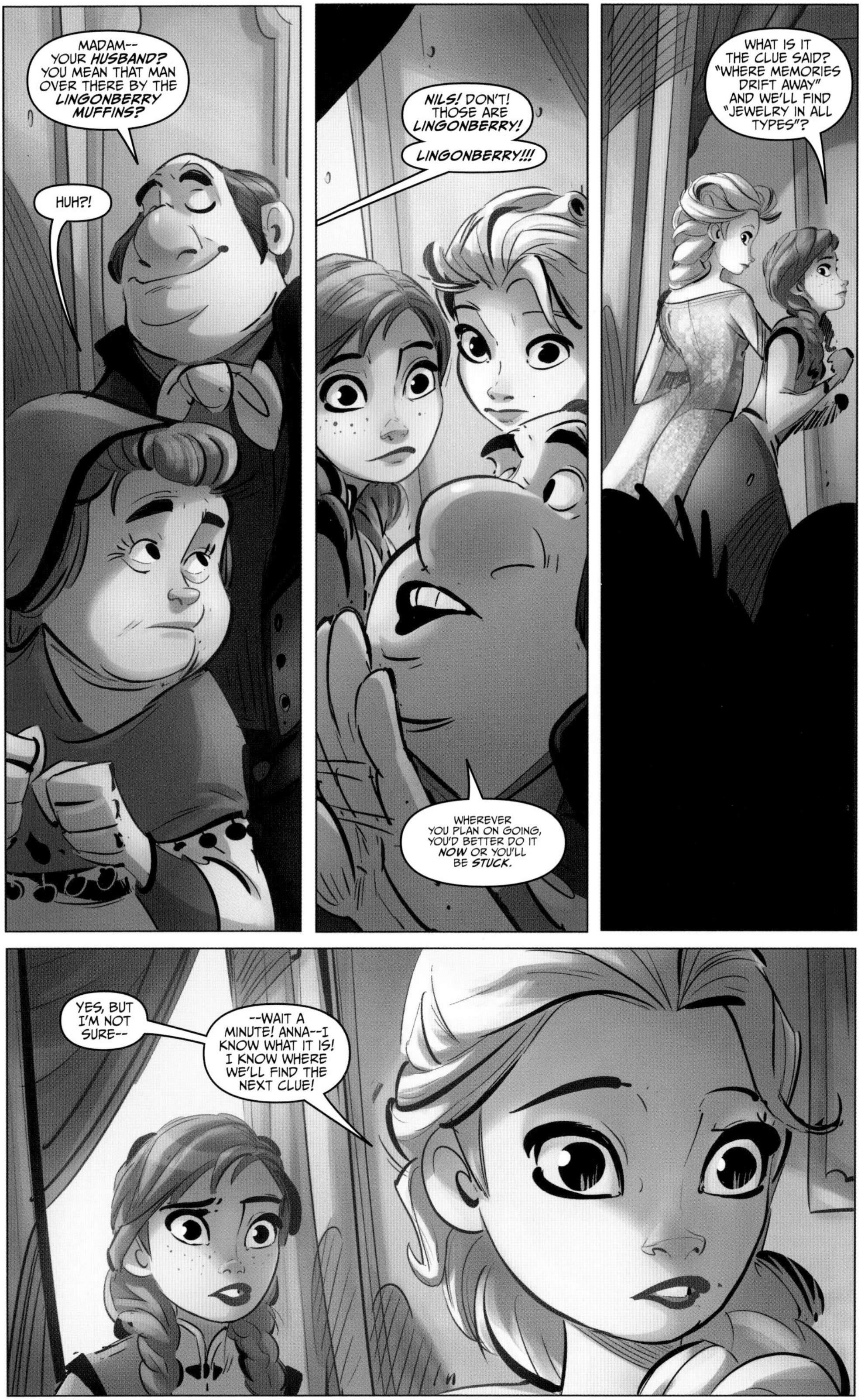
MADAM-- YOUR HUSBAND? YOU MEAN THAT MAN OVER THERE BY THE LINGONBERRY MUFFINS?
HUH?!
NILS! DON'T! THOSE ARE LINGONBERRY!
LINGONBERRY!!!
WHEREVER YOU PLAN ON GOING, YOU'D BETTER DO IT NOW OR YOU'LL BE STUCK.
WHAT IS IT THE CLUE SAID? "WHERE MEMORIES DRIFT AWAY" AND WE'LL FIND "JEWELRY IN ALL TYPES"?
YES, BUT I'M NOT SURE--
--WAIT A MINUTE! ANNA--I KNOW WHAT IT IS! I KNOW WHERE WE'LL FIND THE NEXT CLUE!

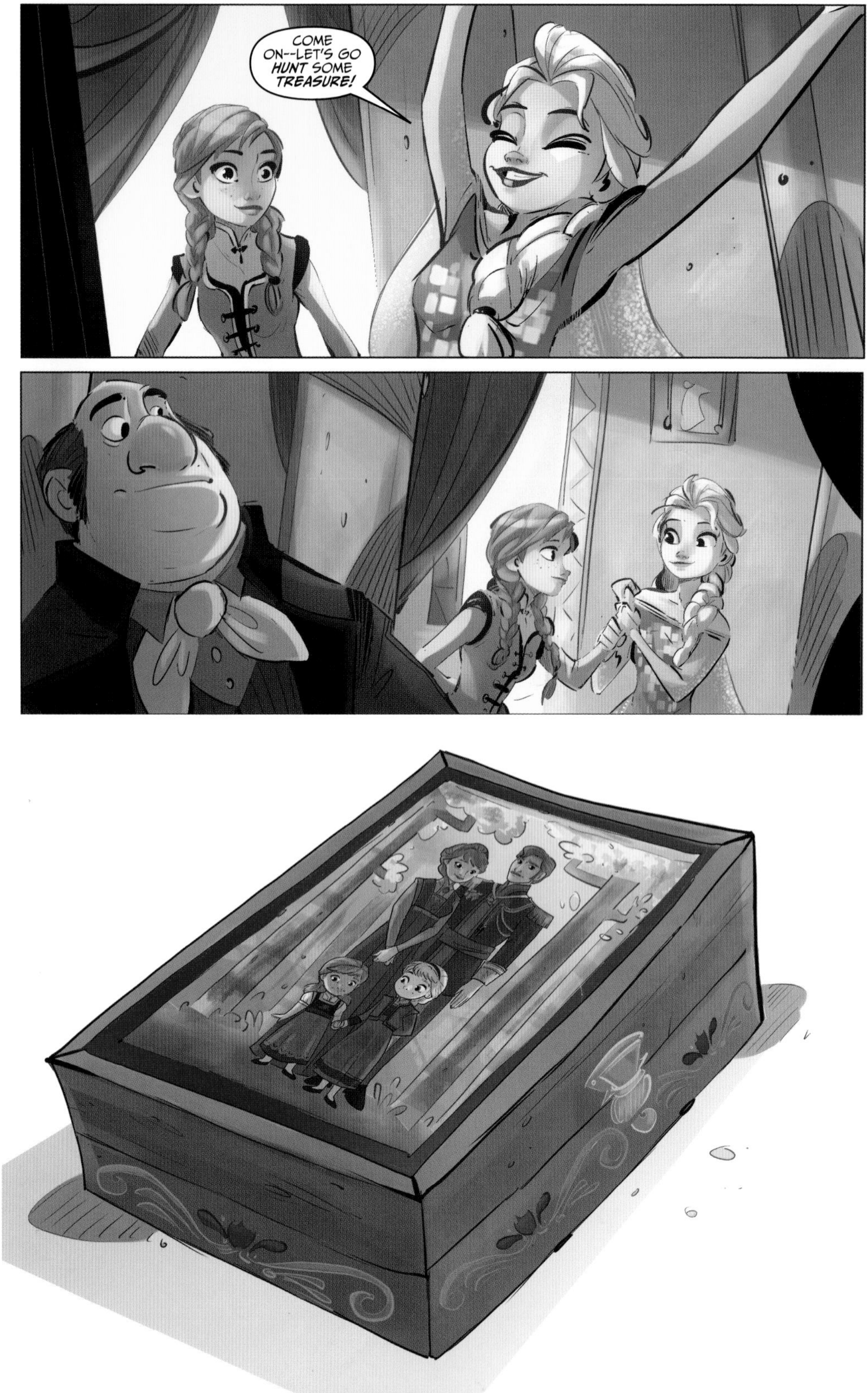
COME ON--LET'S GO HUNT SOME TREASURE!

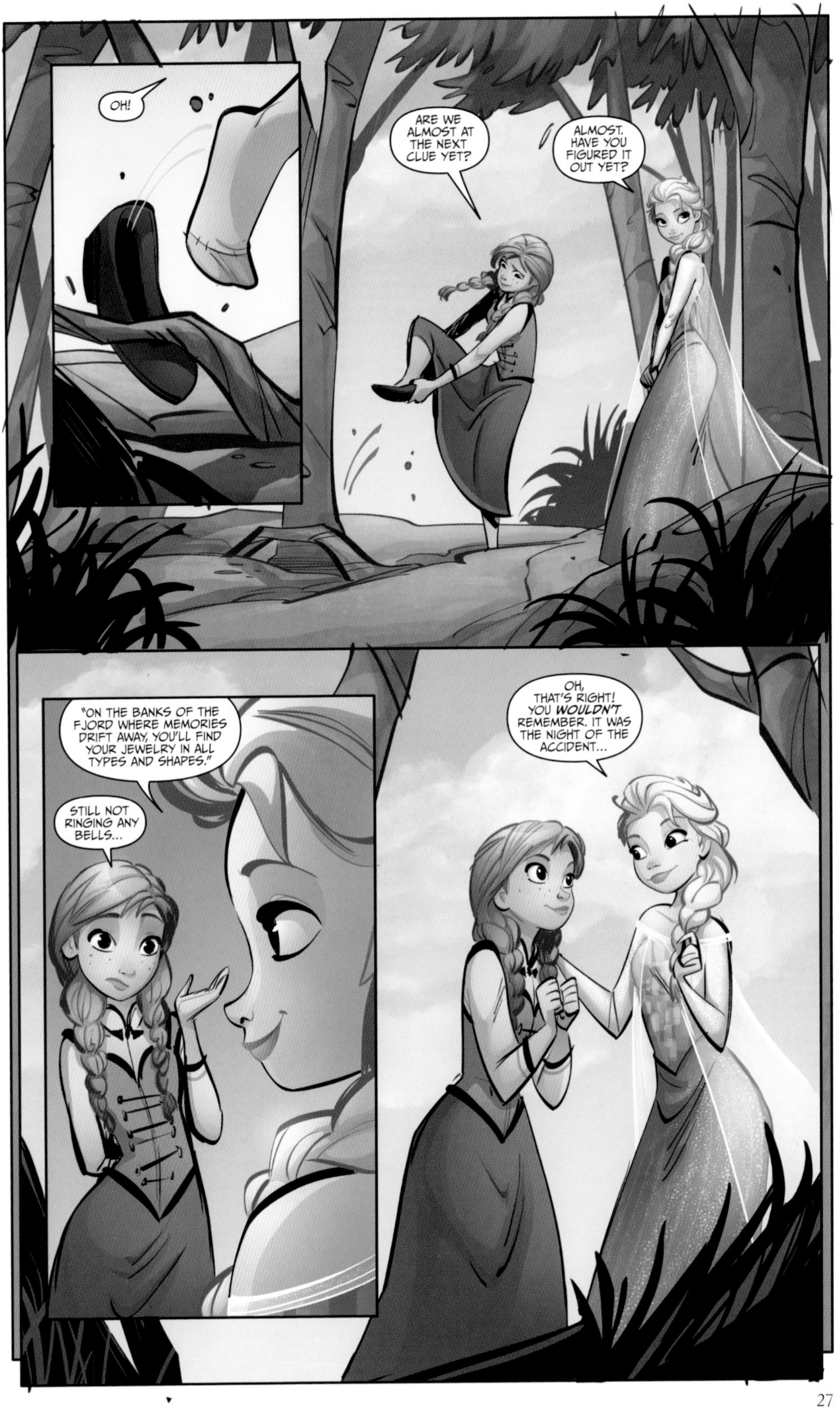
OH!
ARE WE ALMOST AT THE NEXT CLUE YET?
ALMOST. HAVE YOU FIGURED IT OUT YET?
"ON THE BANKS OF THE FJORD WHERE MEMORIES DRIFT AWAY, YOU'LL FIND YOUR JEWELRY IN ALL TYPES AND SHAPES."
STILL NOT RINGING ANY BELLS...
OH, THAT'S RIGHT! YOU *WOULDN'T* REMEMBER. IT WAS THE NIGHT OF THE ACCIDENT...

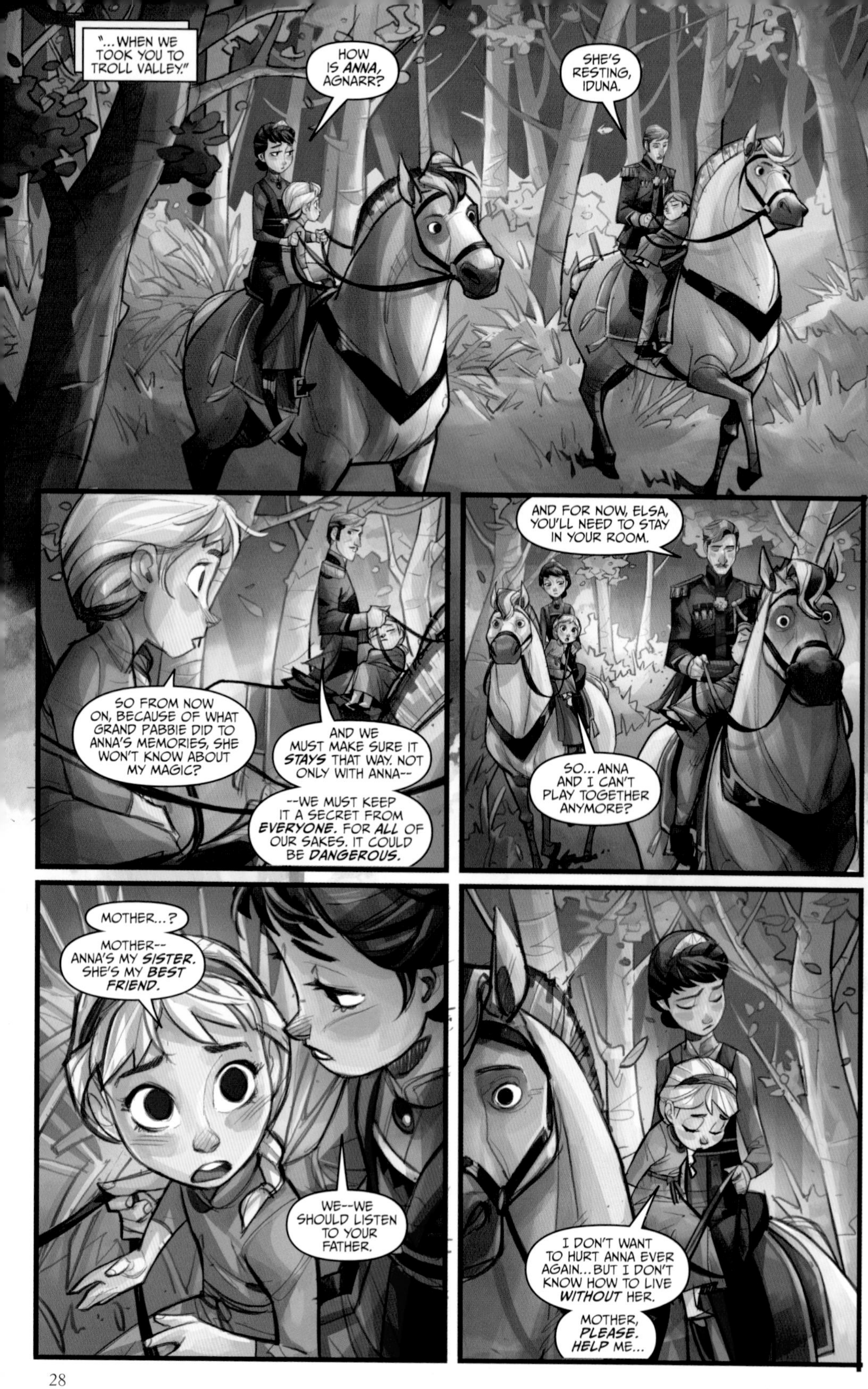
"...WHEN WE TOOK YOU TO TROLL VALLEY."
HOW IS ANNA, AGNARR?
SHE'S RESTING, IDUNA.
SO FROM NOW ON, BECAUSE OF WHAT GRAND PABBIE DID TO ANNA'S MEMORIES, SHE WON'T KNOW ABOUT MY MAGIC?
AND WE MUST MAKE SURE IT STAYS THAT WAY. NOT ONLY WITH ANNA--
--WE MUST KEEP IT A SECRET FROM EVERYONE. FOR ALL OF OUR SAKES. IT COULD BE DANGEROUS.
AND FOR NOW, ELSA, YOU'LL NEED TO STAY IN YOUR ROOM.
SO...ANNA AND I CAN'T PLAY TOGETHER ANYMORE?
MOTHER...?
MOTHER-- ANNA'S MY SISTER. SHE'S MY BEST FRIEND.
WE--WE SHOULD LISTEN TO YOUR FATHER.
I DON'T WANT TO HURT ANNA EVER AGAIN...BUT I DON'T KNOW HOW TO LIVE WITHOUT HER.
MOTHER, PLEASE. HELP ME...

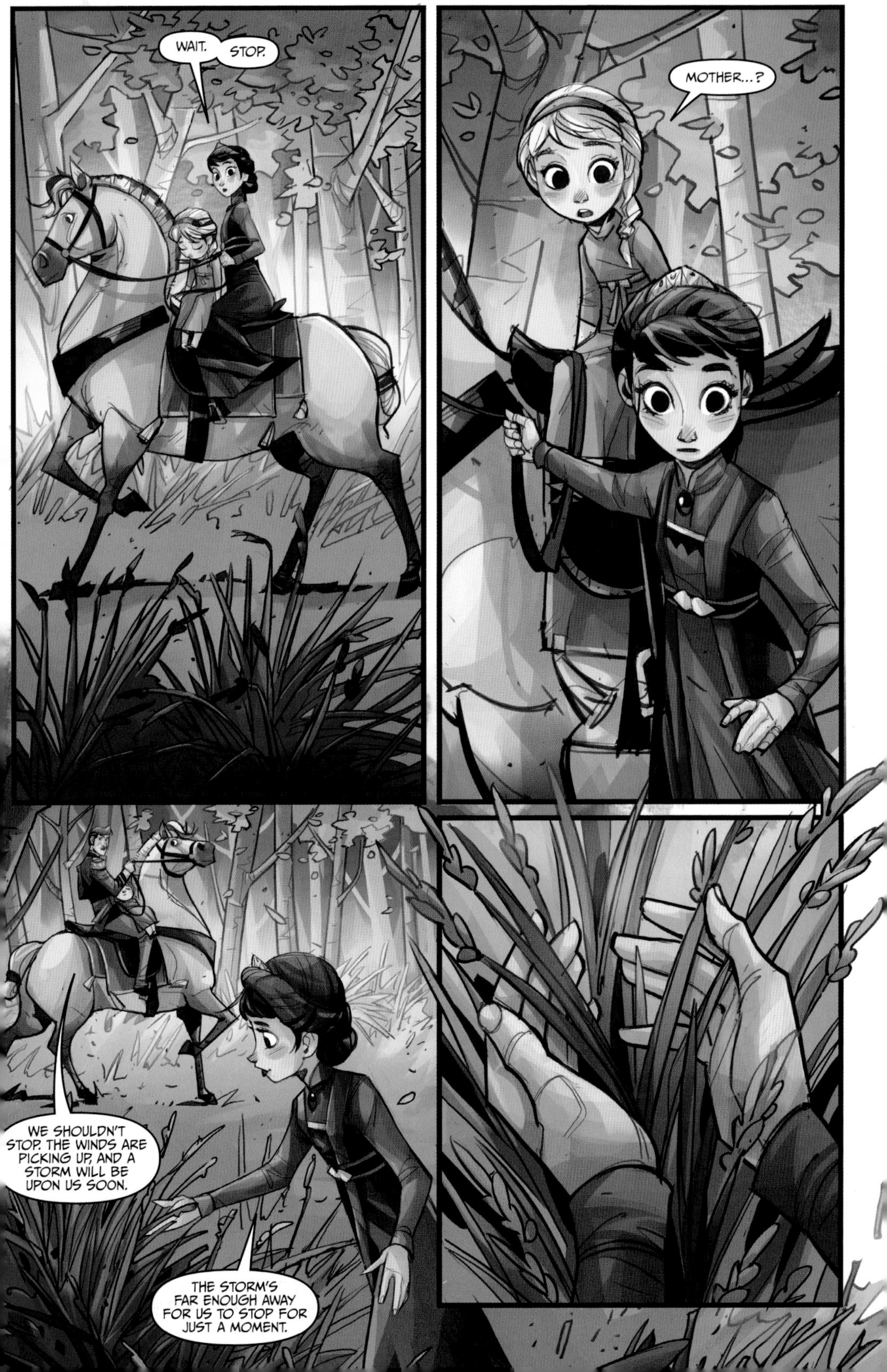
WAIT.
STOP.
MOTHER...?
WE SHOULDN'T STOP. THE WINDS ARE PICKING UP, AND A STORM WILL BE UPON US SOON.
THE STORM'S FAR ENOUGH AWAY FOR US TO STOP FOR JUST A MOMENT.

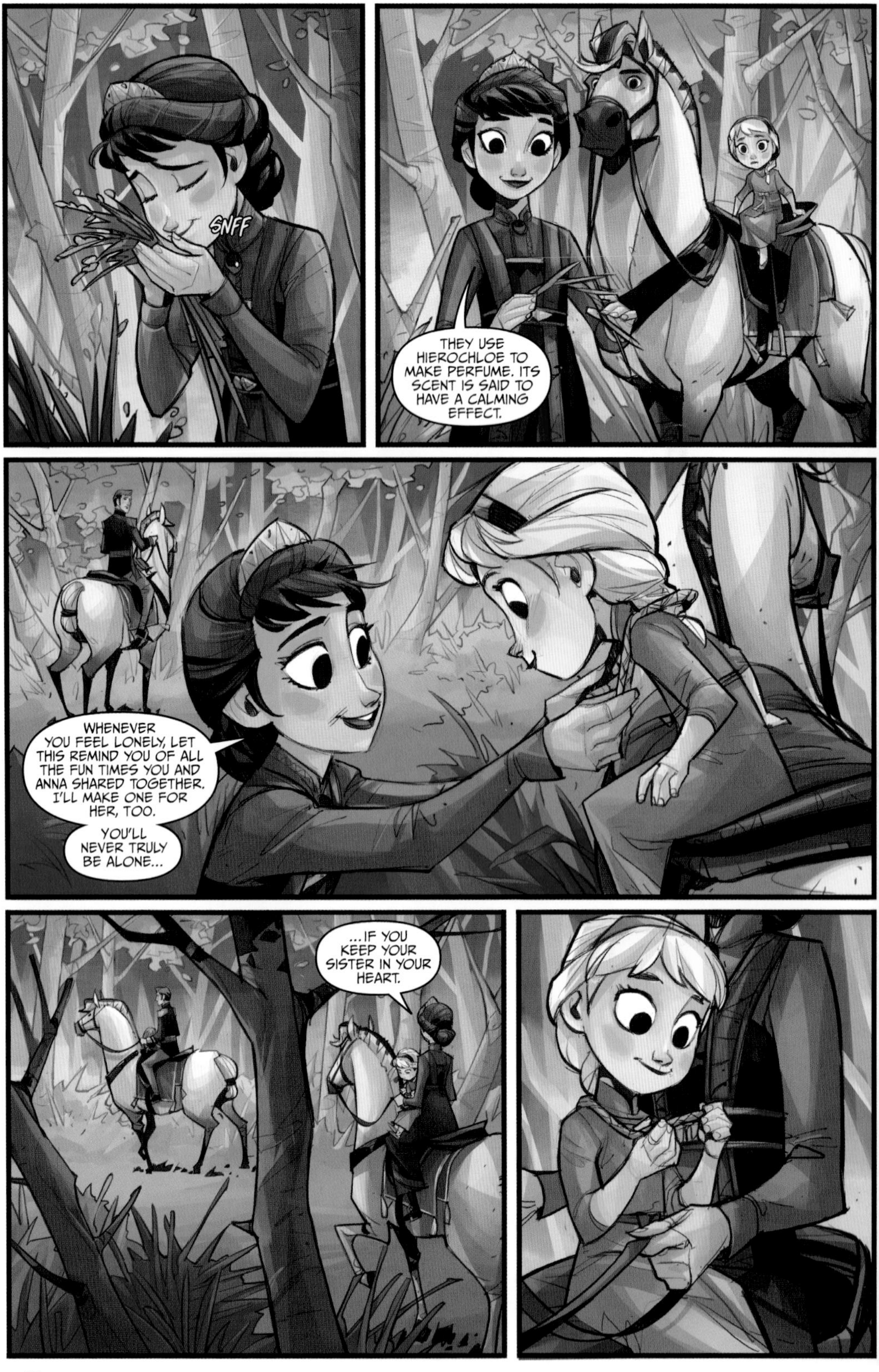
SNFF
THEY USE HIEROCHLOE TO MAKE PERFUME. ITS SCENT IS SAID TO HAVE A CALMING EFFECT.
WHENEVER YOU FEEL LONELY, LET THIS REMIND YOU OF ALL THE FUN TIMES YOU AND ANNA SHARED TOGETHER. I'LL MAKE ONE FOR HER, TOO.
YOU'LL NEVER TRULY BE ALONE...
...IF YOU KEEP YOUR SISTER IN YOUR HEART.

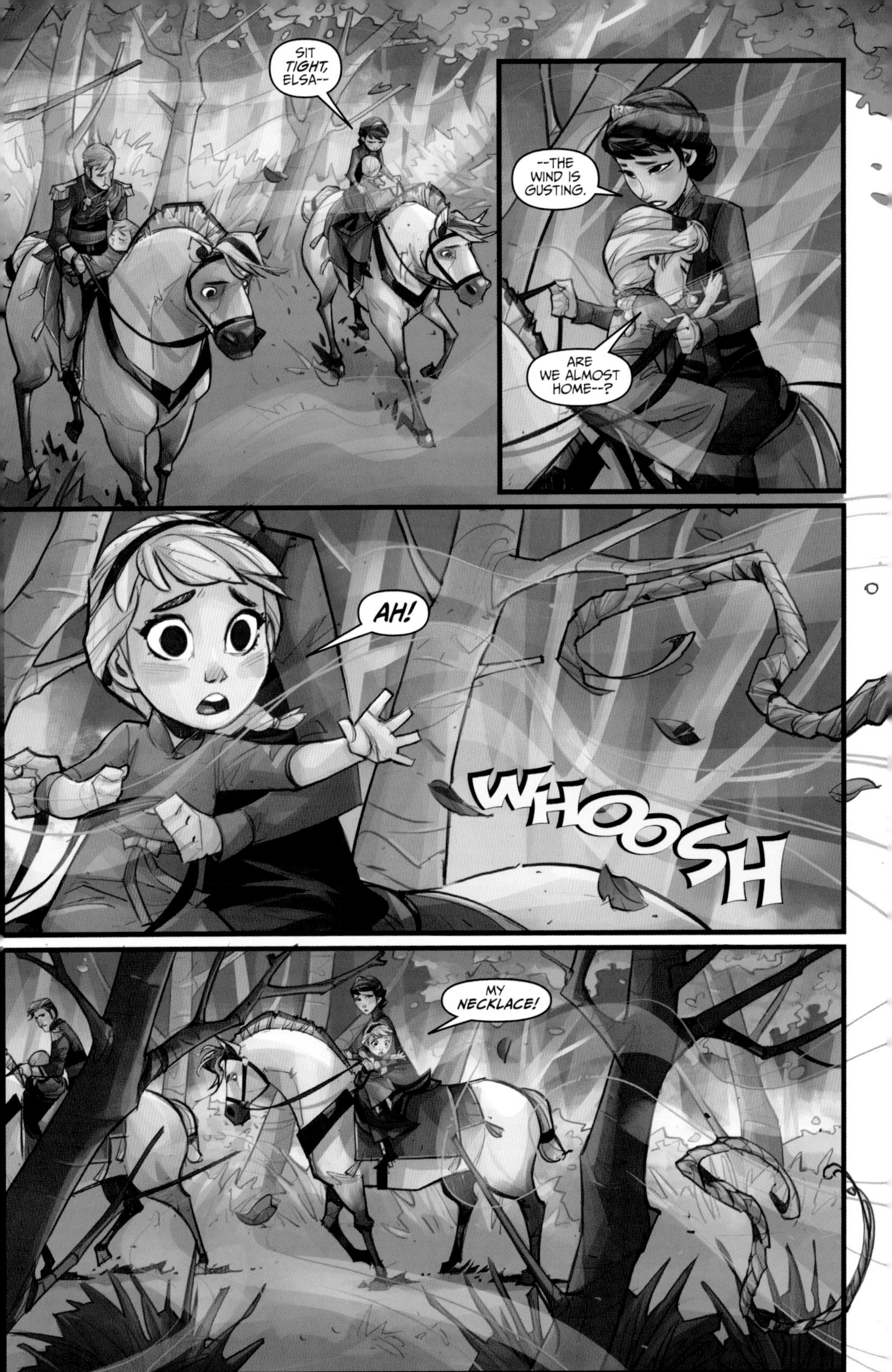
SIT TIGHT, ELSA--
--THE WIND IS GUSTING.
ARE WE ALMOST HOME--?
AH!
WHOOSH
MY NECKLACE!

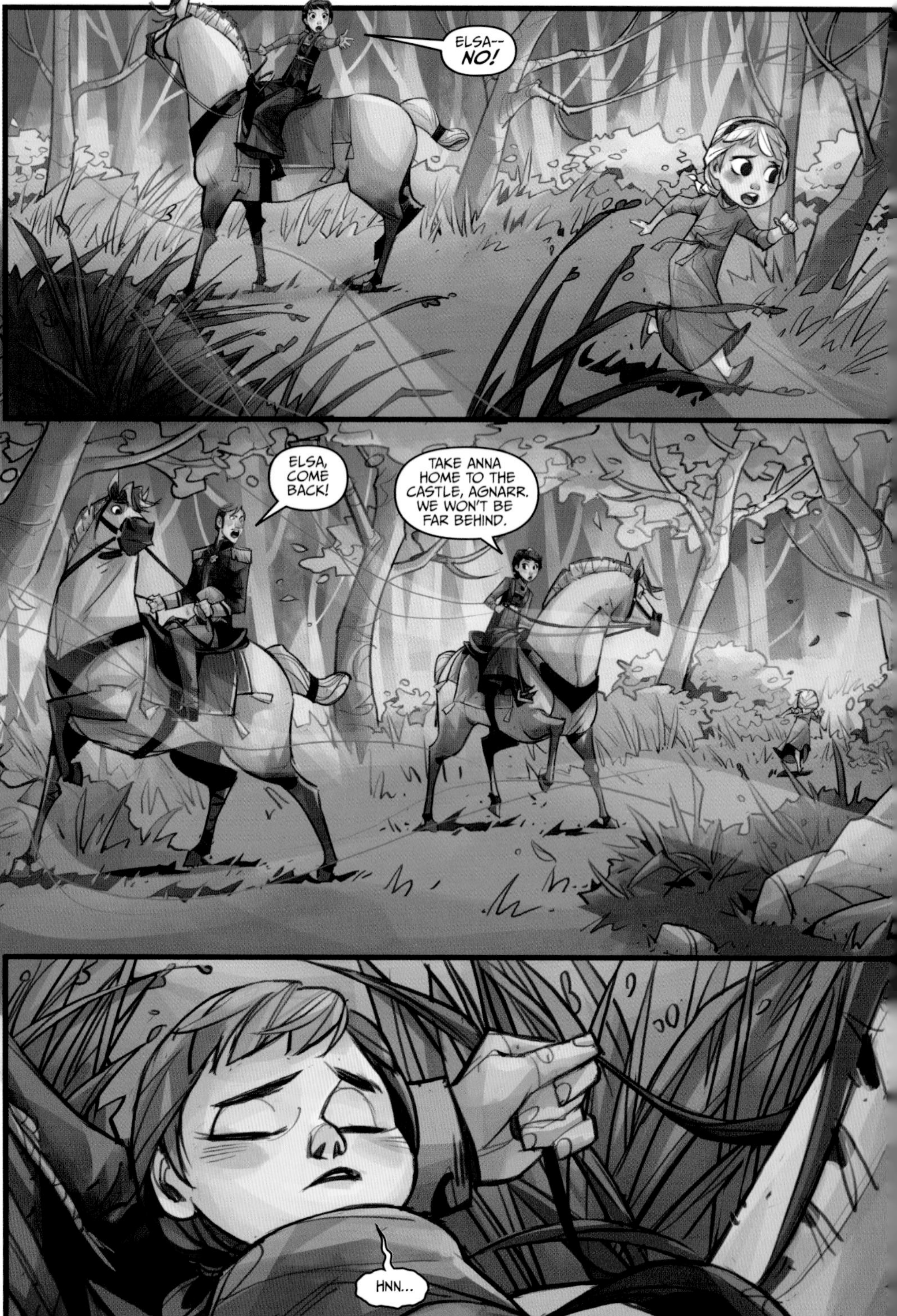
ELSA-- NO!
ELSA, COME BACK!
TAKE ANNA HOME TO THE CASTLE, AGNARR. WE WON'T BE FAR BEHIND.
HNN...

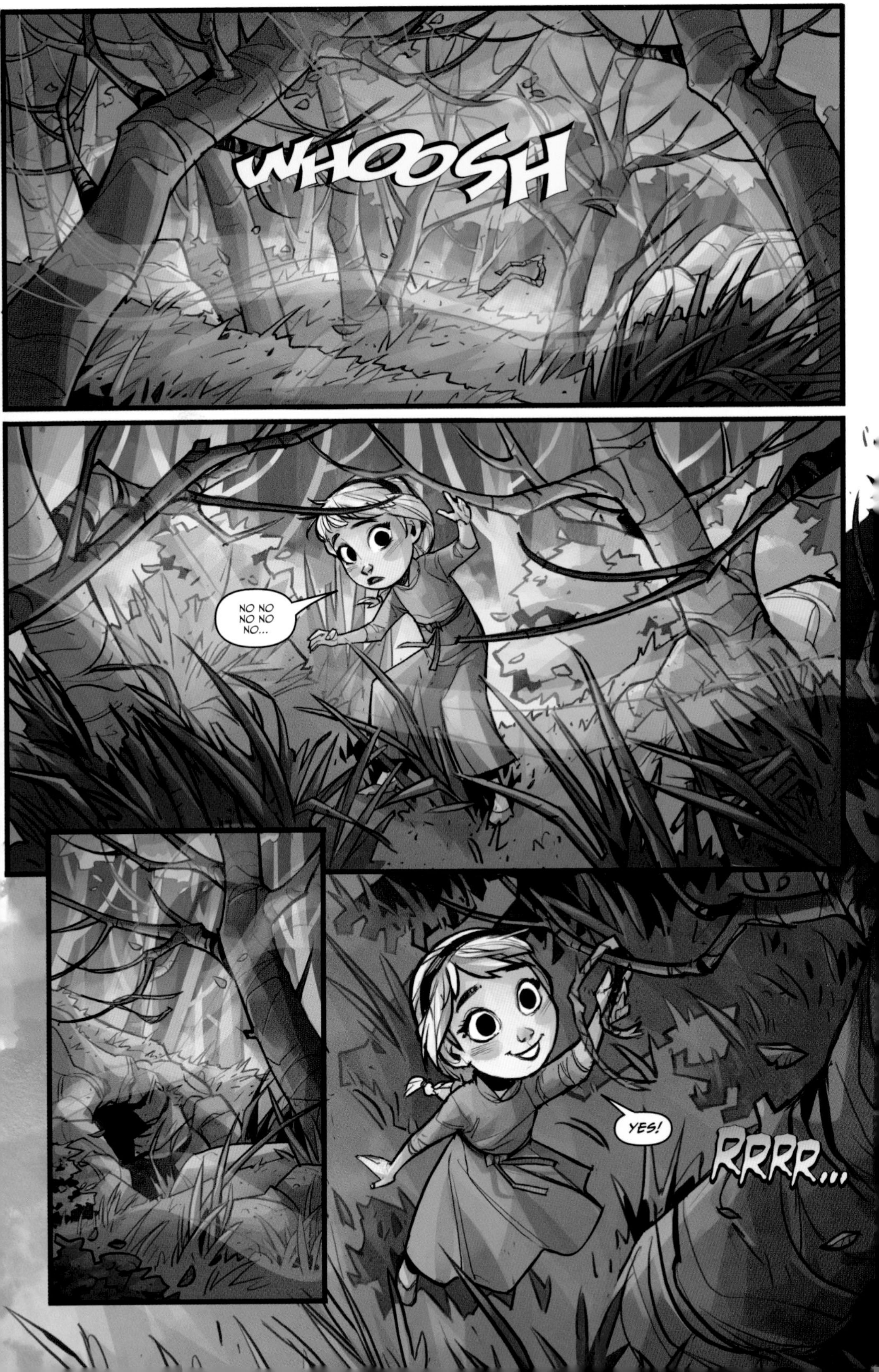
WHOOSH
NO NO NO NO NO...
YES!
RRRR...

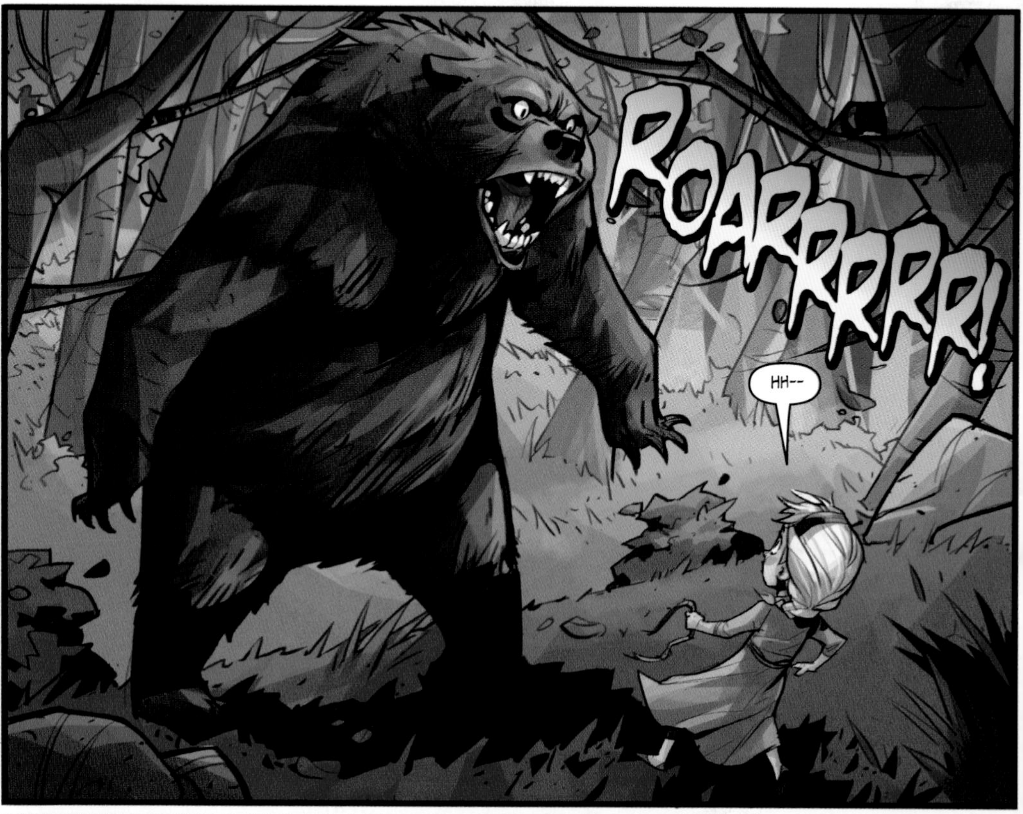
ROARRRRRR!
HH--

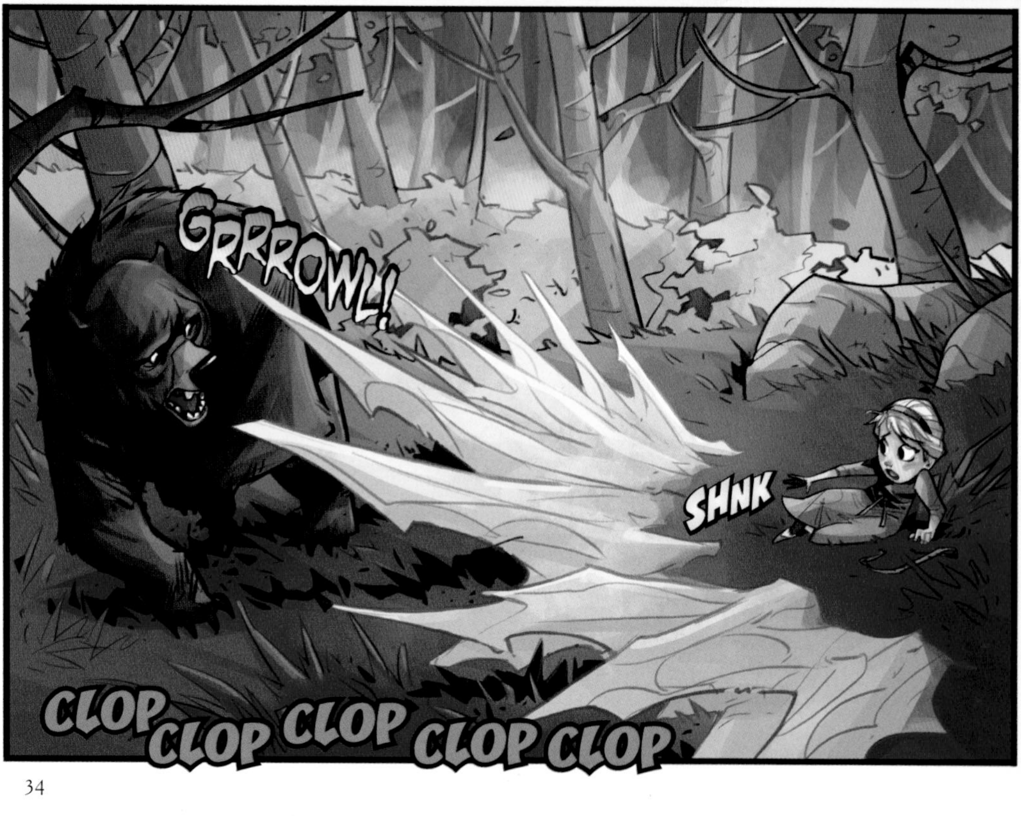
GRRROWL!
SHNK
CLOP CLOP CLOP CLOP CLOP

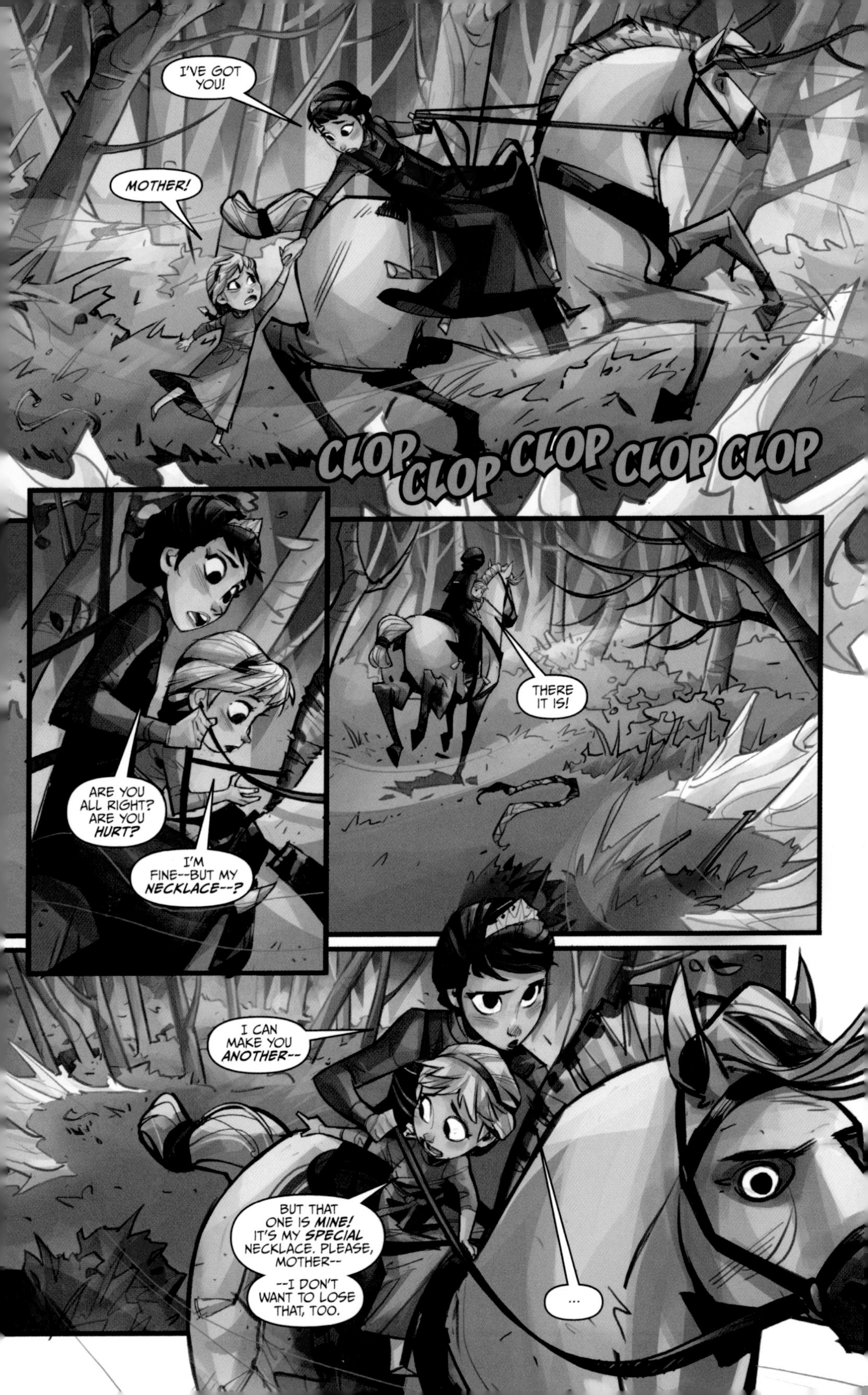
I'VE GOT YOU!
MOTHER!
CLOP CLOP CLOP CLOP CLOP
ARE YOU ALL RIGHT? ARE YOU HURT?
I'M FINE--BUT MY NECKLACE--?
THERE IT IS!
I CAN MAKE YOU ANOTHER--
BUT THAT ONE IS MINE! IT'S MY SPECIAL NECKLACE. PLEASE, MOTHER--
--I DON'T WANT TO LOSE THAT, TOO.
...

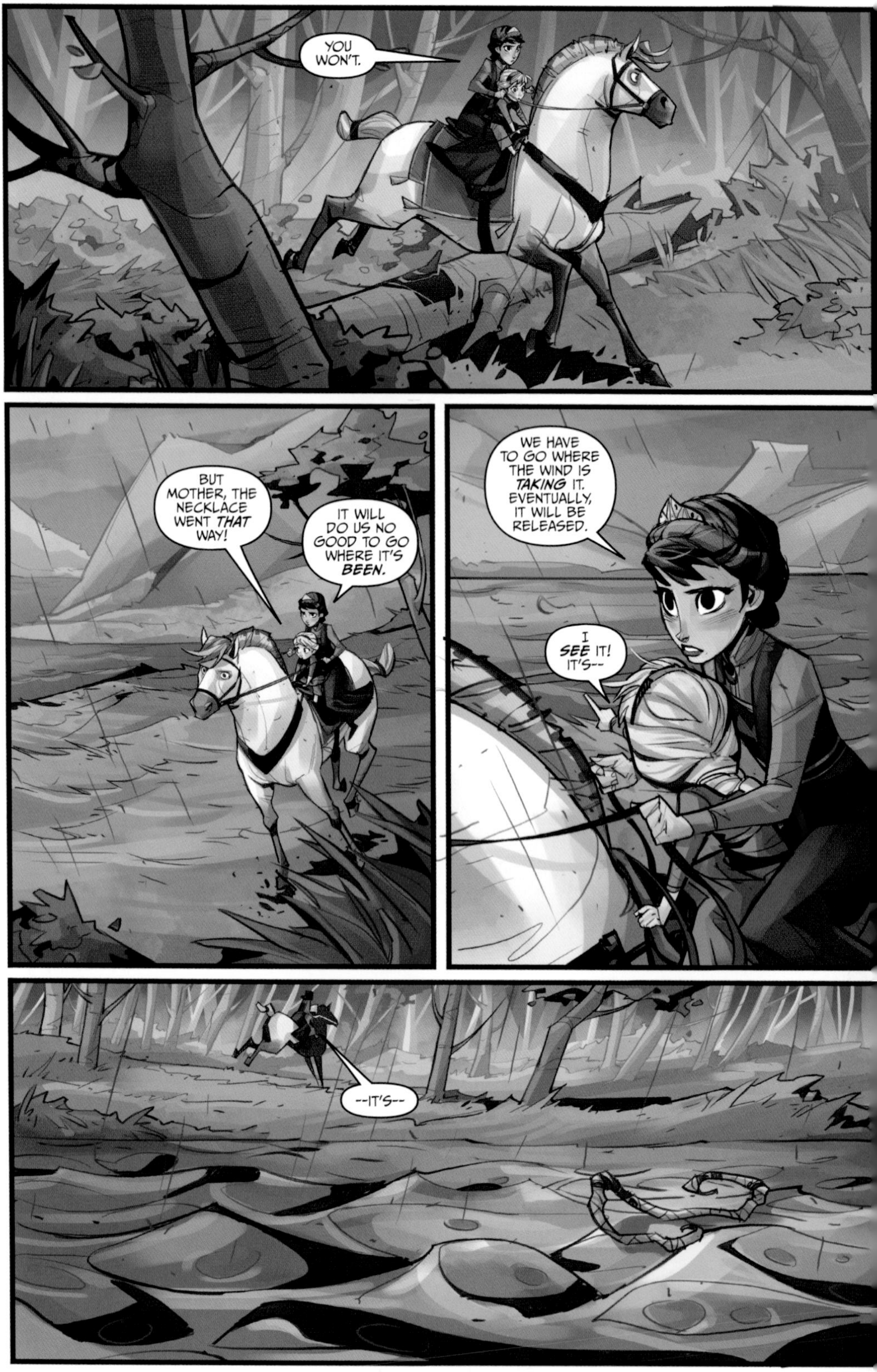
YOU WON'T.
BUT MOTHER, THE NECKLACE WENT THAT WAY!
IT WILL DO US NO GOOD TO GO WHERE IT'S BEEN.
WE HAVE TO GO WHERE THE WIND IS TAKING IT. EVENTUALLY, IT WILL BE RELEASED.
I SEE IT! IT'S--
--IT'S--

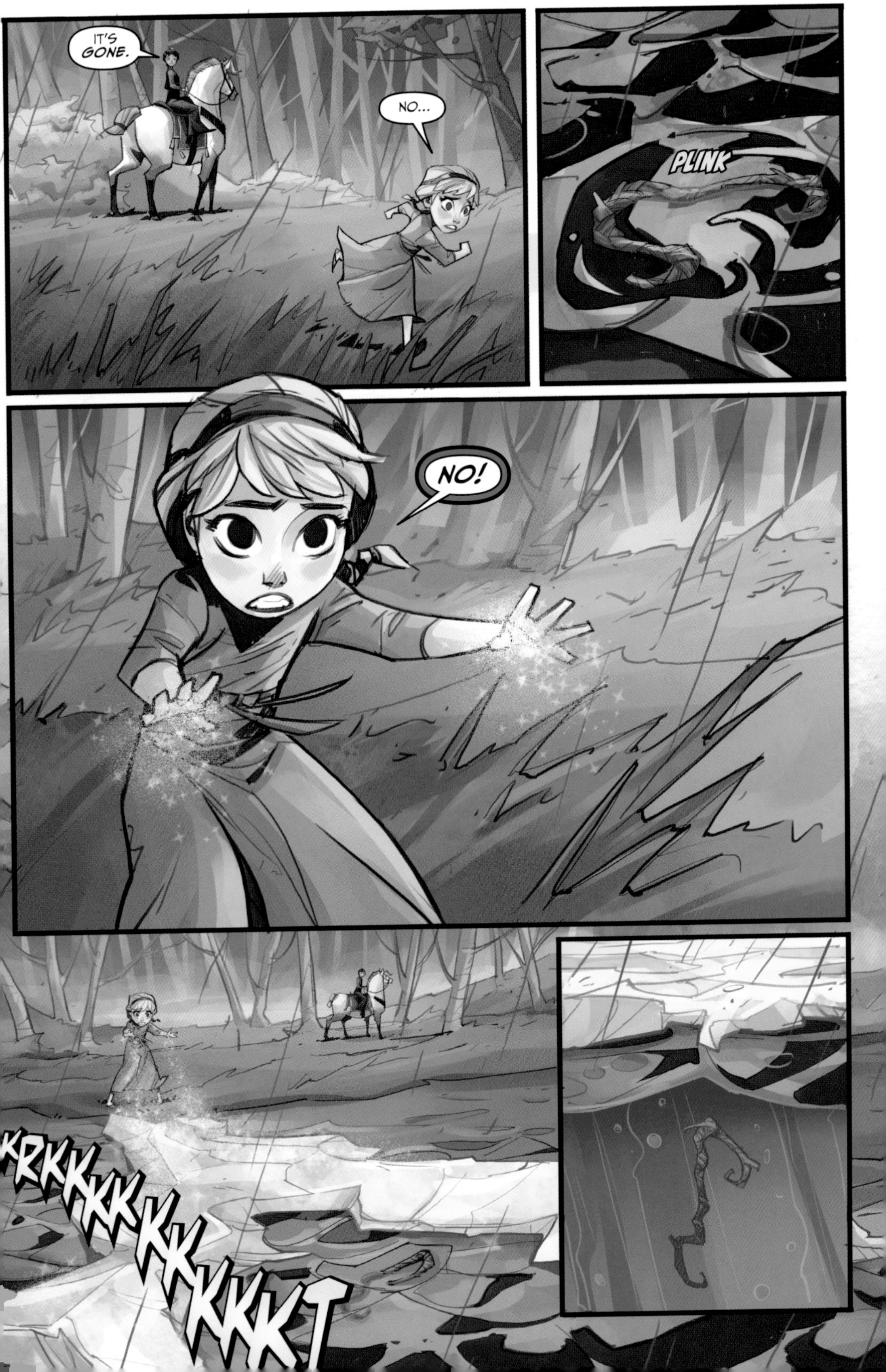
IT'S GONE.
NO...
PLINK
NO!
KRKKKKKKKKKT

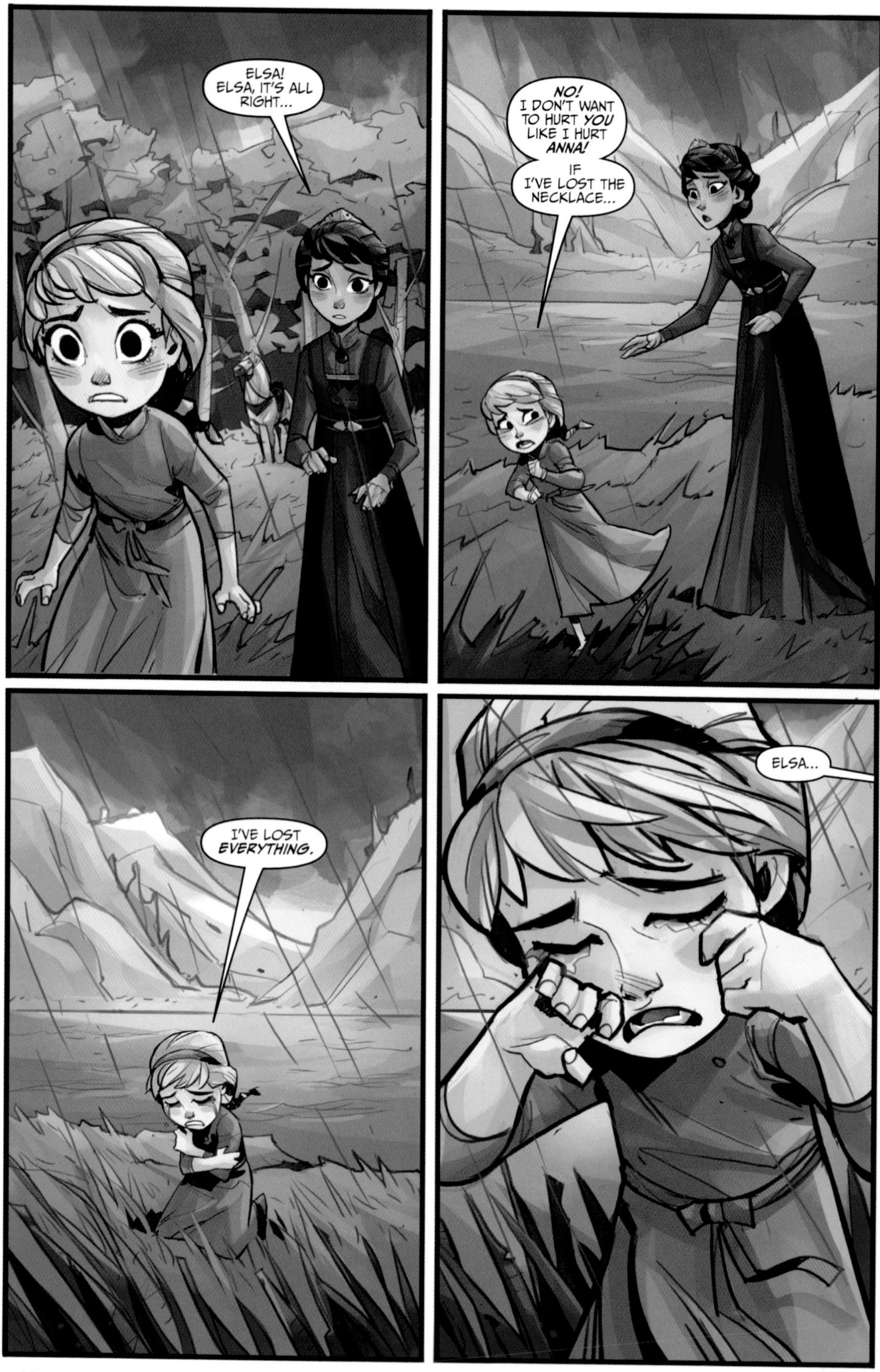
ELSA! ELSA, IT'S ALL RIGHT...
NO! I DON'T WANT TO HURT YOU LIKE I HURT ANNA!
IF I'VE LOST THE NECKLACE...
I'VE LOST EVERYTHING.
ELSA...

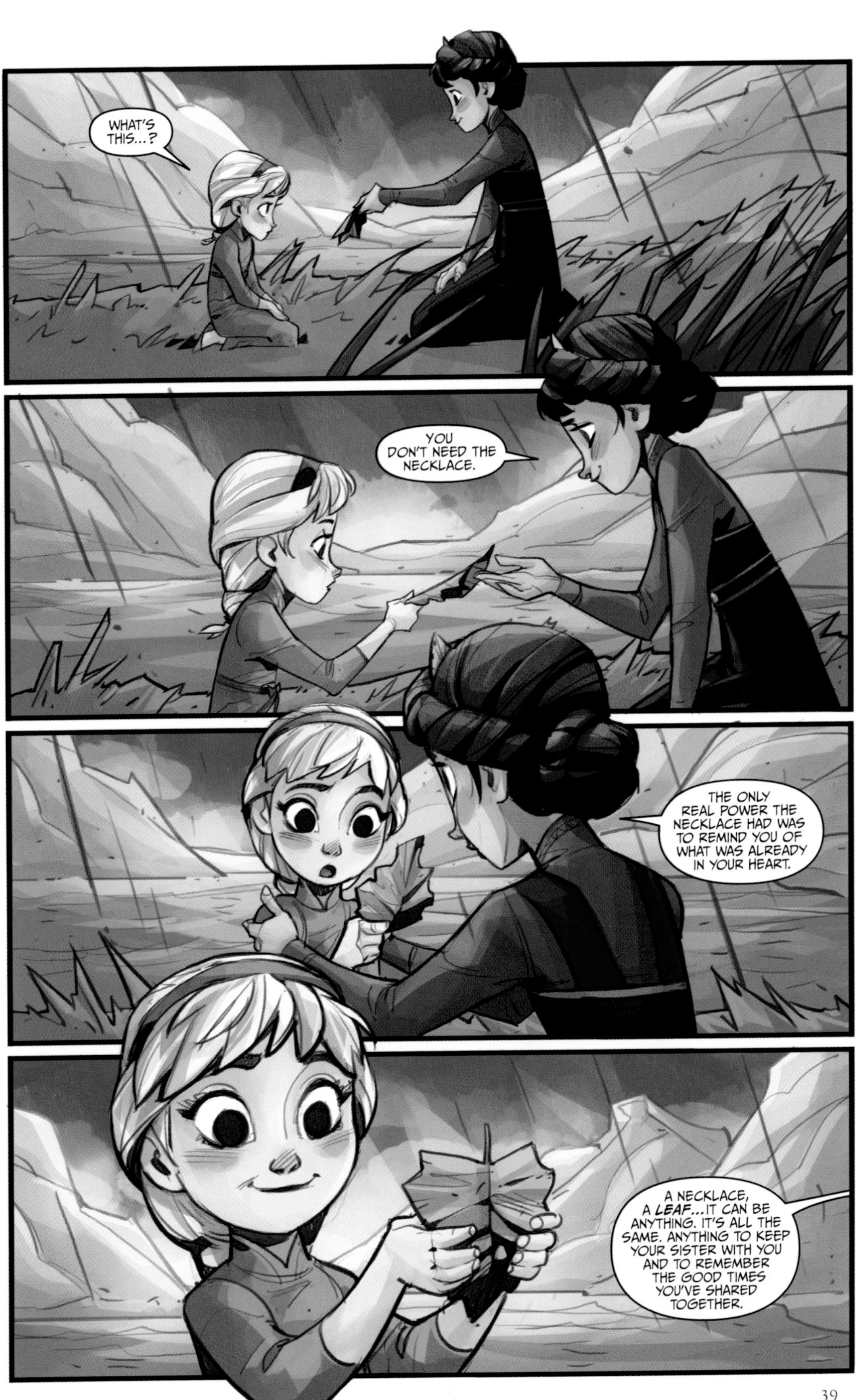
WHAT'S THIS...?
YOU DON'T NEED THE NECKLACE.
THE ONLY REAL POWER THE NECKLACE HAD WAS TO REMIND YOU OF WHAT WAS ALREADY IN YOUR HEART.
A NECKLACE, A ***LEAF***...IT CAN BE ANYTHING. IT'S ALL THE SAME. ANYTHING TO KEEP YOUR SISTER WITH YOU AND TO REMEMBER THE GOOD TIMES YOU'VE SHARED TOGETHER.

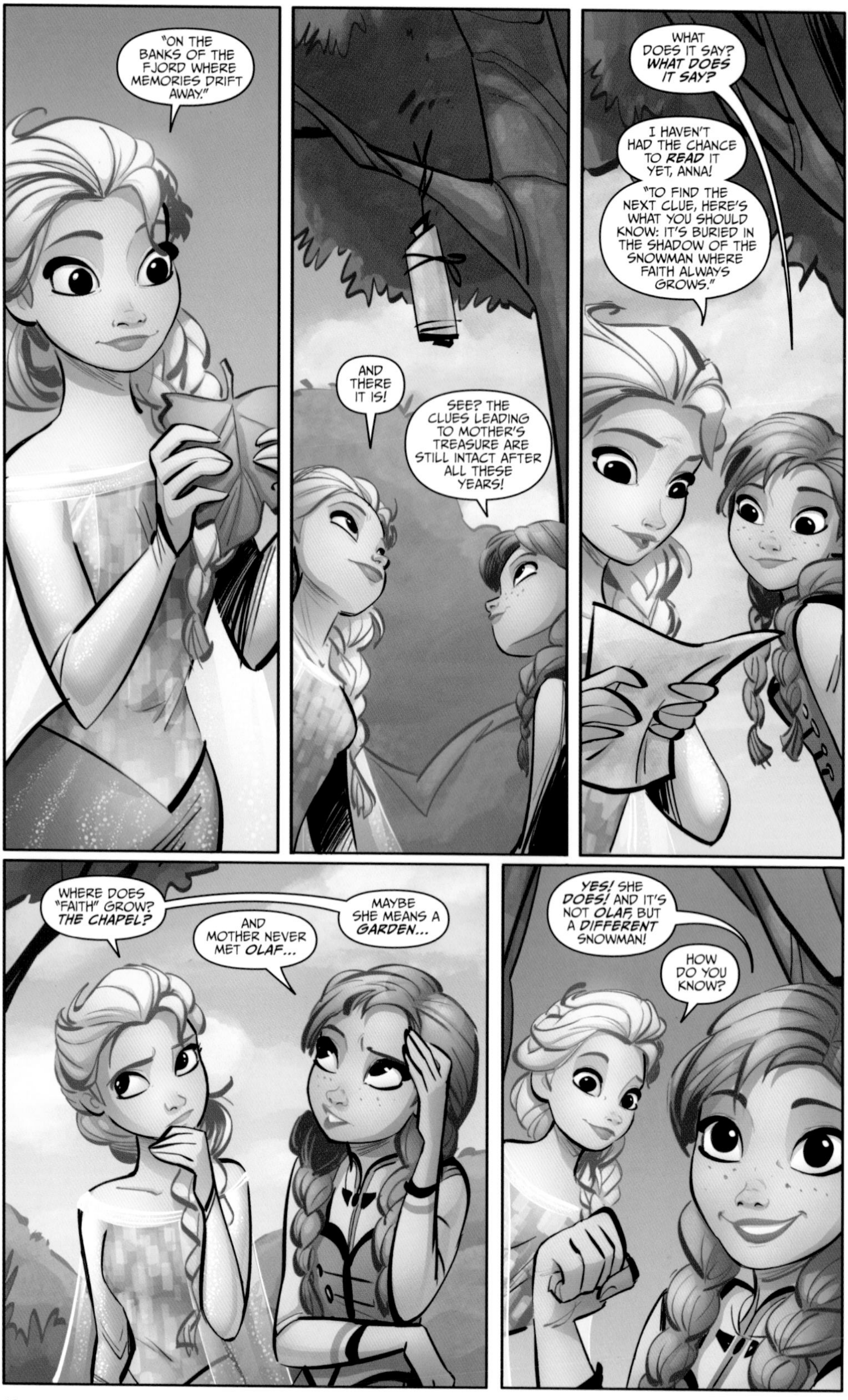
"ON THE BANKS OF THE FJORD WHERE MEMORIES DRIFT AWAY."
AND THERE IT IS!
SEE? THE CLUES LEADING TO MOTHER'S TREASURE ARE STILL INTACT AFTER ALL THESE YEARS!
WHAT DOES IT SAY? WHAT DOES IT SAY?
I HAVEN'T HAD THE CHANCE TO READ IT YET, ANNA!
"TO FIND THE NEXT CLUE, HERE'S WHAT YOU SHOULD KNOW: IT'S BURIED IN THE SHADOW OF THE SNOWMAN WHERE FAITH ALWAYS GROWS."
WHERE DOES "FAITH" GROW? THE CHAPEL?
MAYBE SHE MEANS A GARDEN...
AND MOTHER NEVER MET OLAF...
YES! SHE DOES! AND IT'S NOT OLAF, BUT A DIFFERENT SNOWMAN!
HOW DO YOU KNOW?

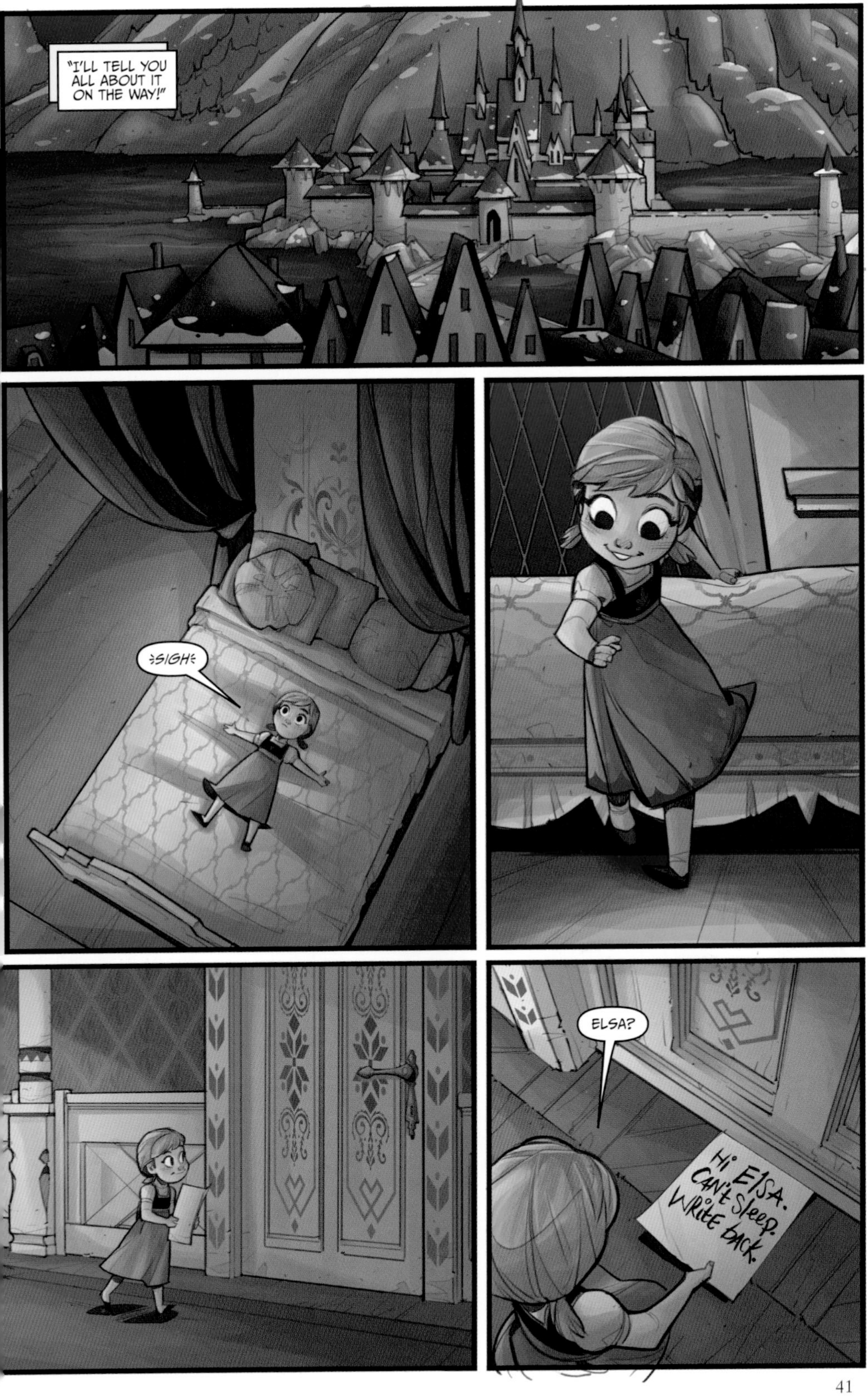
"I'LL TELL YOU ALL ABOUT IT ON THE WAY!"
SIGH
ELSA?
Hi Elsa. Can't sleep. Write back.

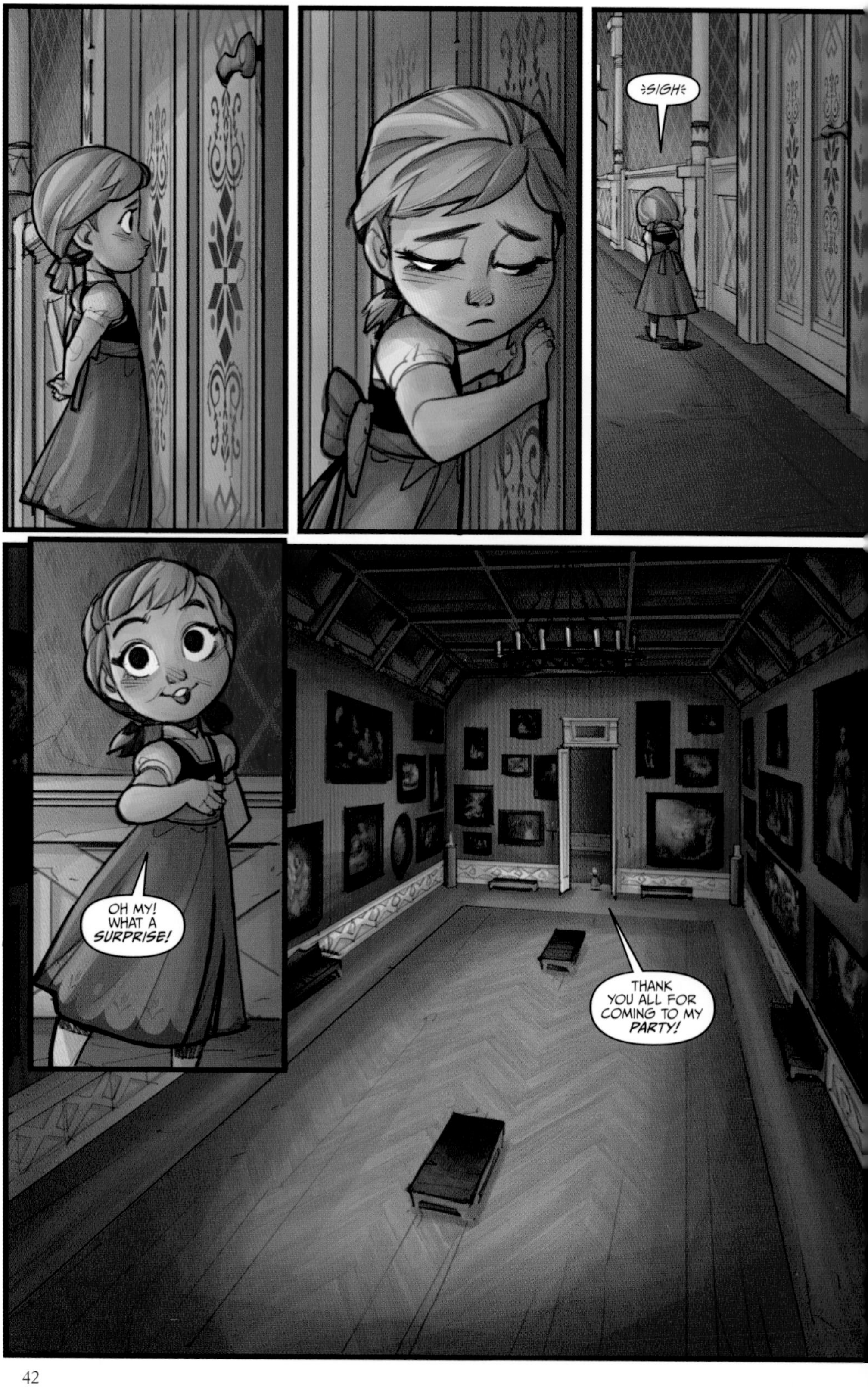
SIGH
OH MY! WHAT A SURPRISE!
THANK YOU ALL FOR COMING TO MY PARTY!

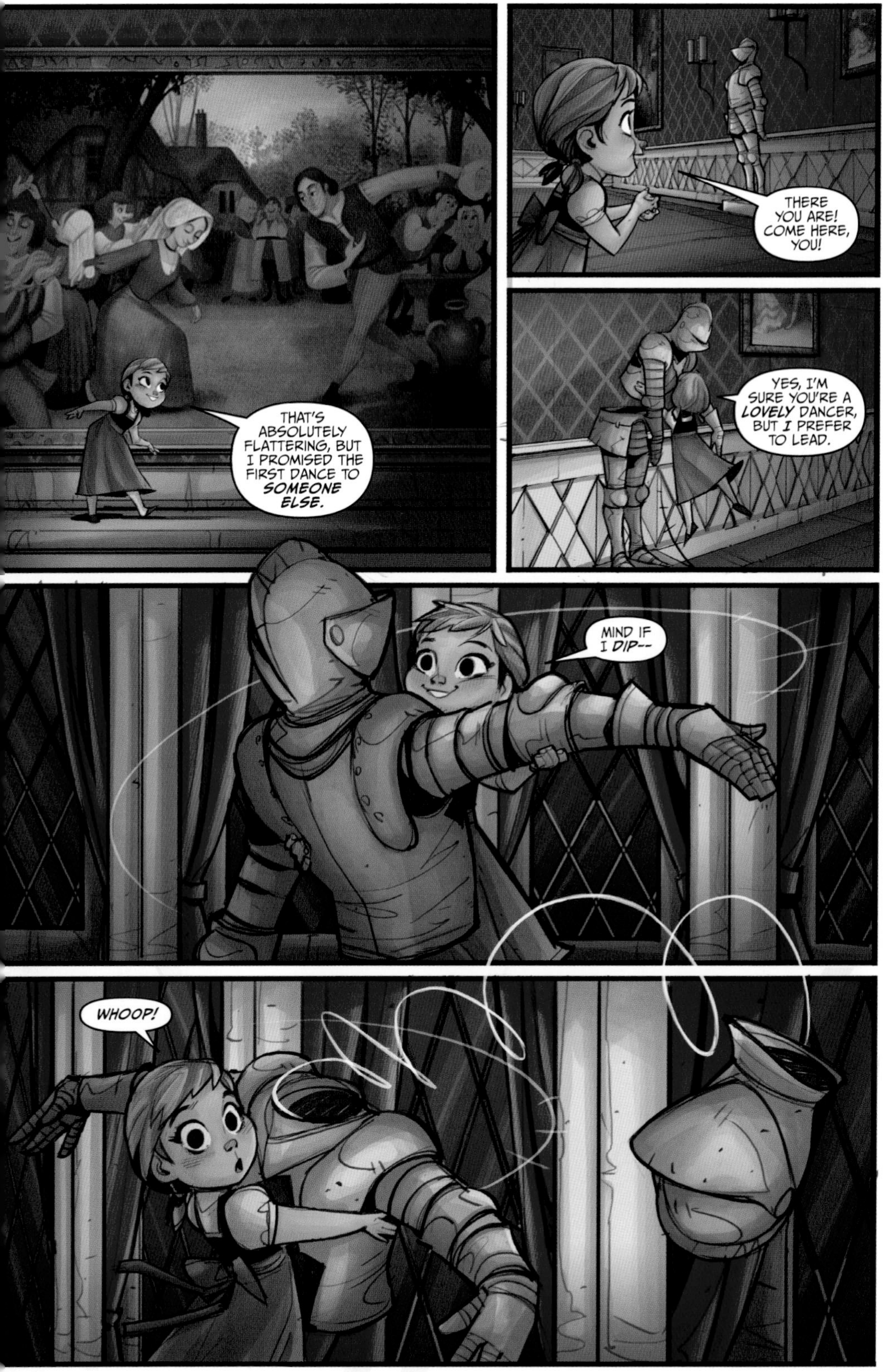
THAT'S ABSOLUTELY FLATTERING, BUT I PROMISED THE FIRST DANCE TO SOMEONE ELSE.
THERE YOU ARE! COME HERE, YOU!
YES, I'M SURE YOU'RE A LOVELY DANCER, BUT I PREFER TO LEAD.
MIND IF I DIP--
WHOOP!

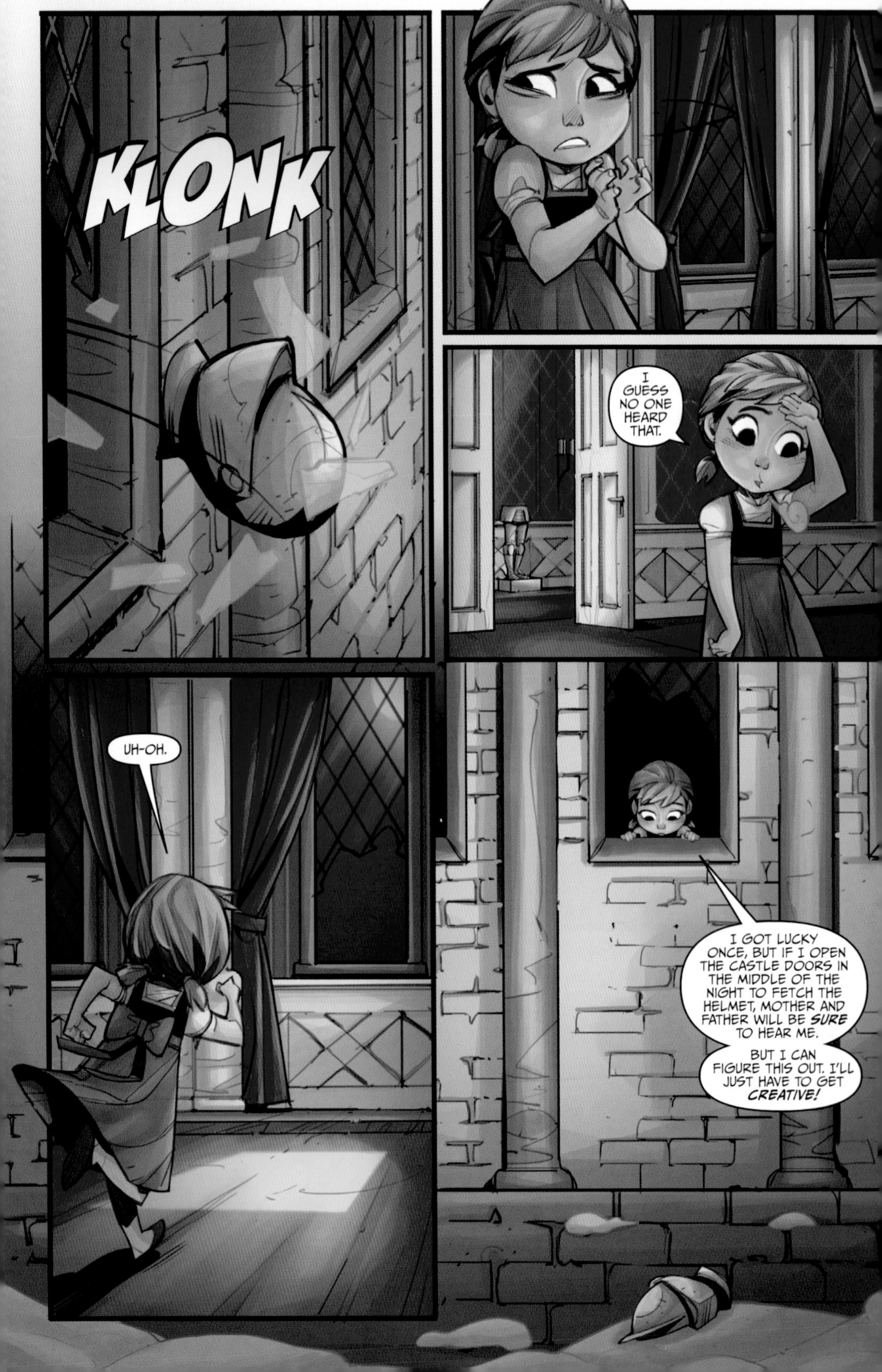
KLONK
I GUESS NO ONE HEARD THAT.
UH-OH.
I GOT LUCKY ONCE, BUT IF I OPEN THE CASTLE DOORS IN THE MIDDLE OF THE NIGHT TO FETCH THE HELMET, MOTHER AND FATHER WILL BE SURE TO HEAR ME.
BUT I CAN FIGURE THIS OUT. I'LL JUST HAVE TO GET CREATIVE!

COME ON... JUST A LITTLE MORE...
MISSED AGAIN!
THERE IT IS! I THINK I'VE...
CLANG
WELL, NOW WHAT?

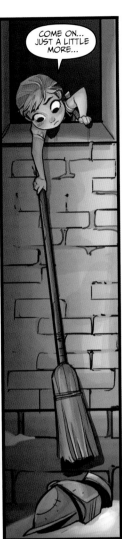

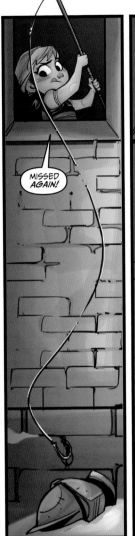

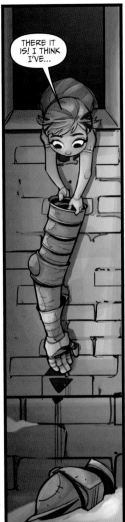

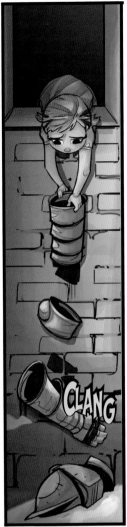

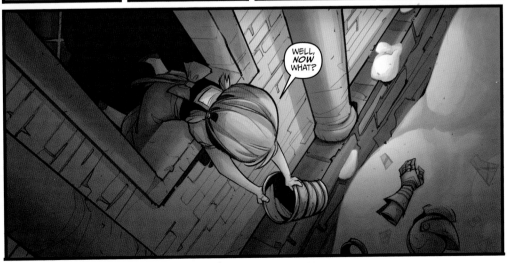

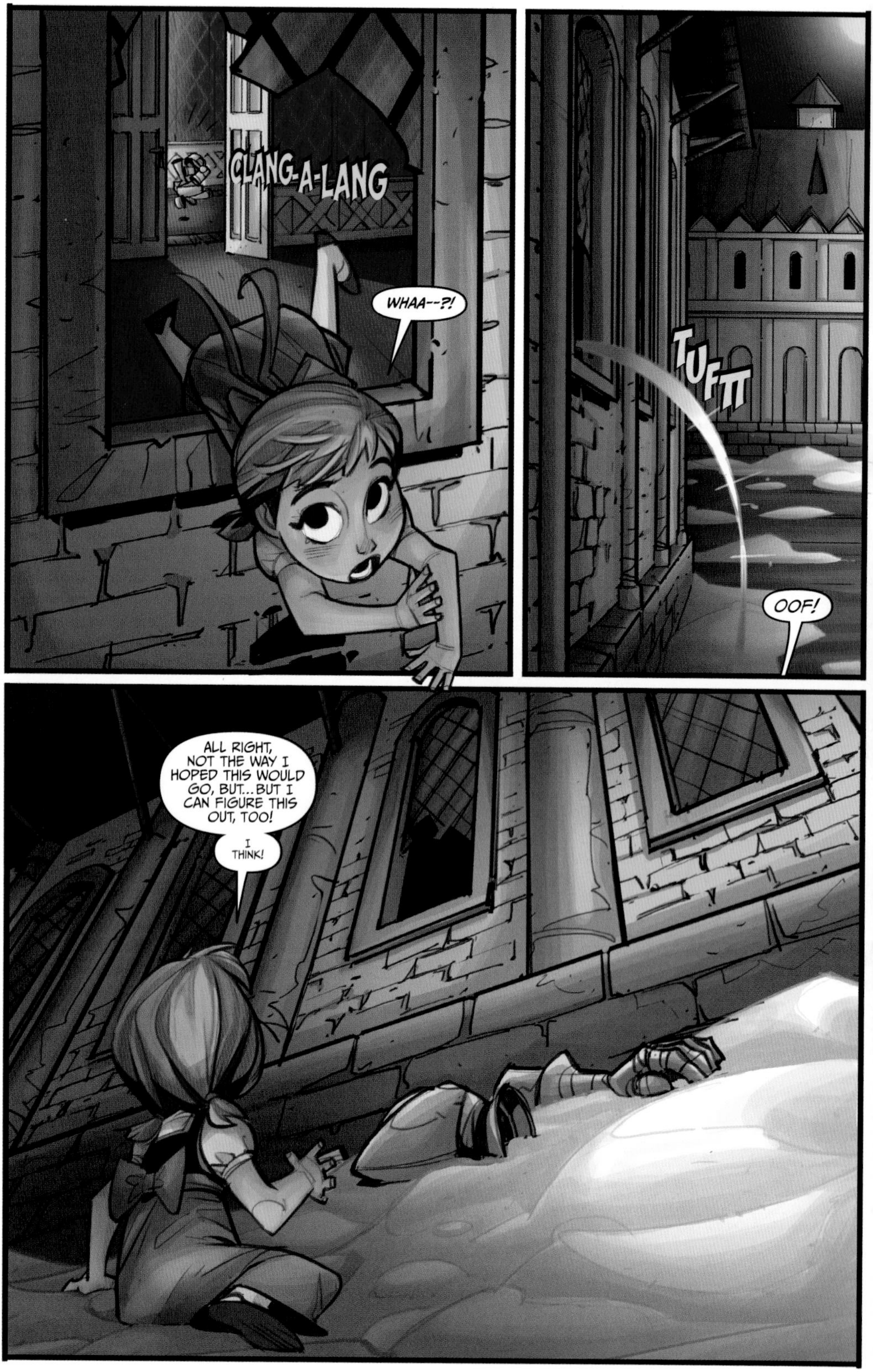
CLANG-A-LANG
WHAA--?!
TUFTT
OOF!
ALL RIGHT, NOT THE WAY I HOPED THIS WOULD GO, BUT...BUT I CAN FIGURE THIS OUT, TOO!
I THINK!

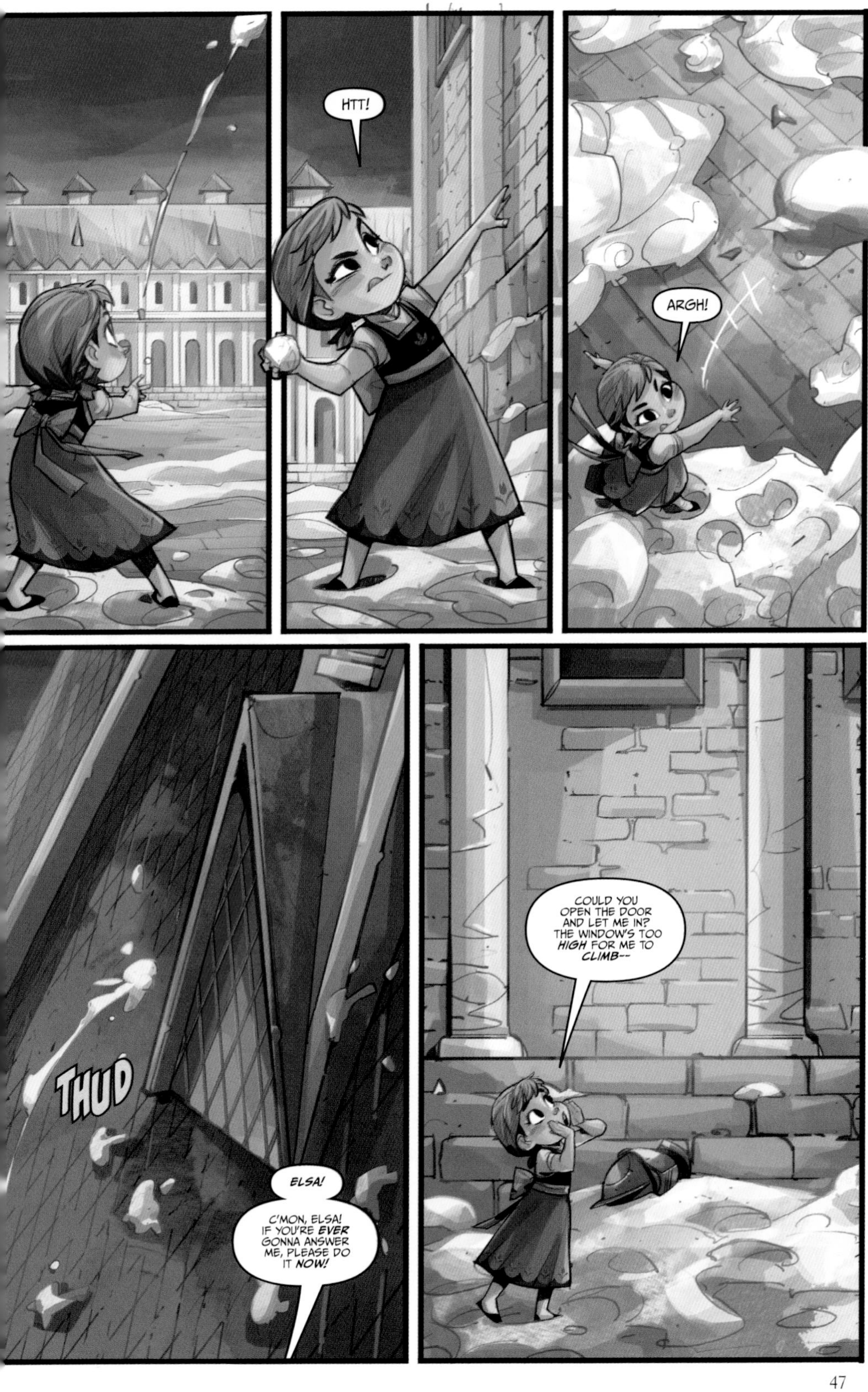
HTT!
ARGH!
THUD
ELSA!
C'MON, ELSA! IF YOU'RE EVER GONNA ANSWER ME, PLEASE DO IT NOW!
COULD YOU OPEN THE DOOR AND LET ME IN? THE WINDOW'S TOO HIGH FOR ME TO CLIMB--

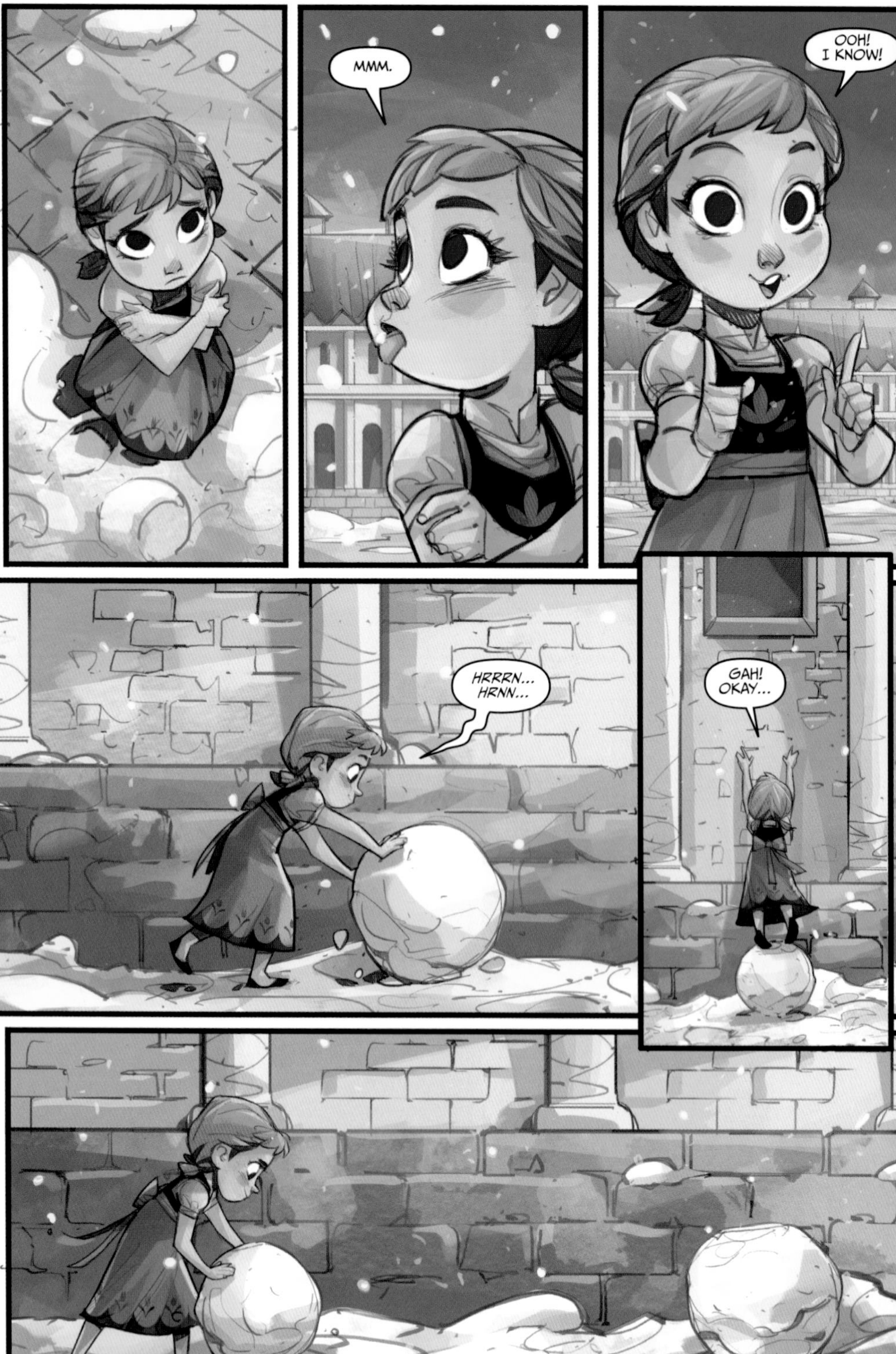
MMM.
OOH! I KNOW!
HRRRN... HRNN...
GAH! OKAY...

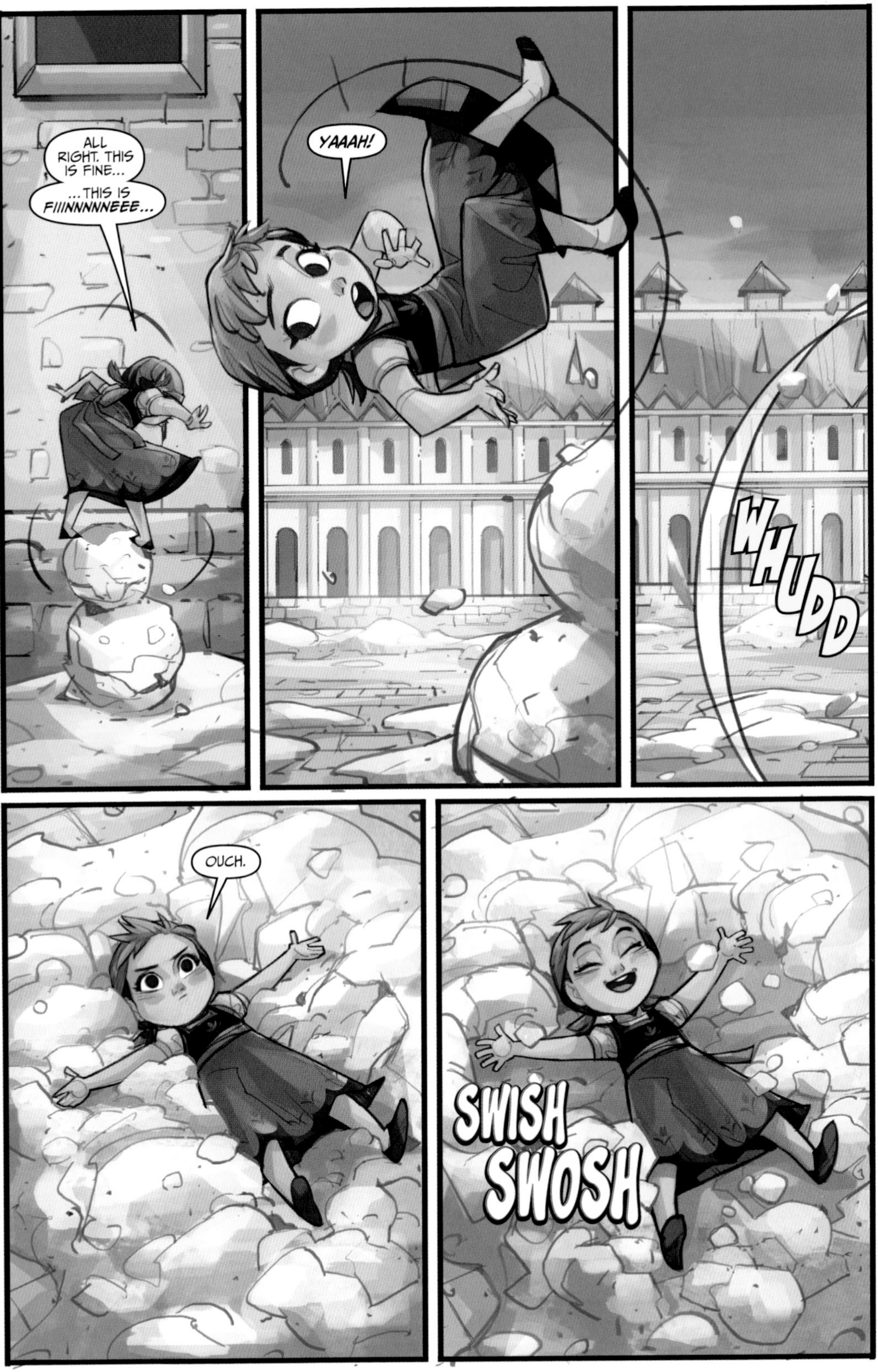
ALL RIGHT. THIS IS FINE...
...THIS IS FIIINNNNNEEE...
YAAAH!
WHUDD
OUCH.
SWISH SWOSH

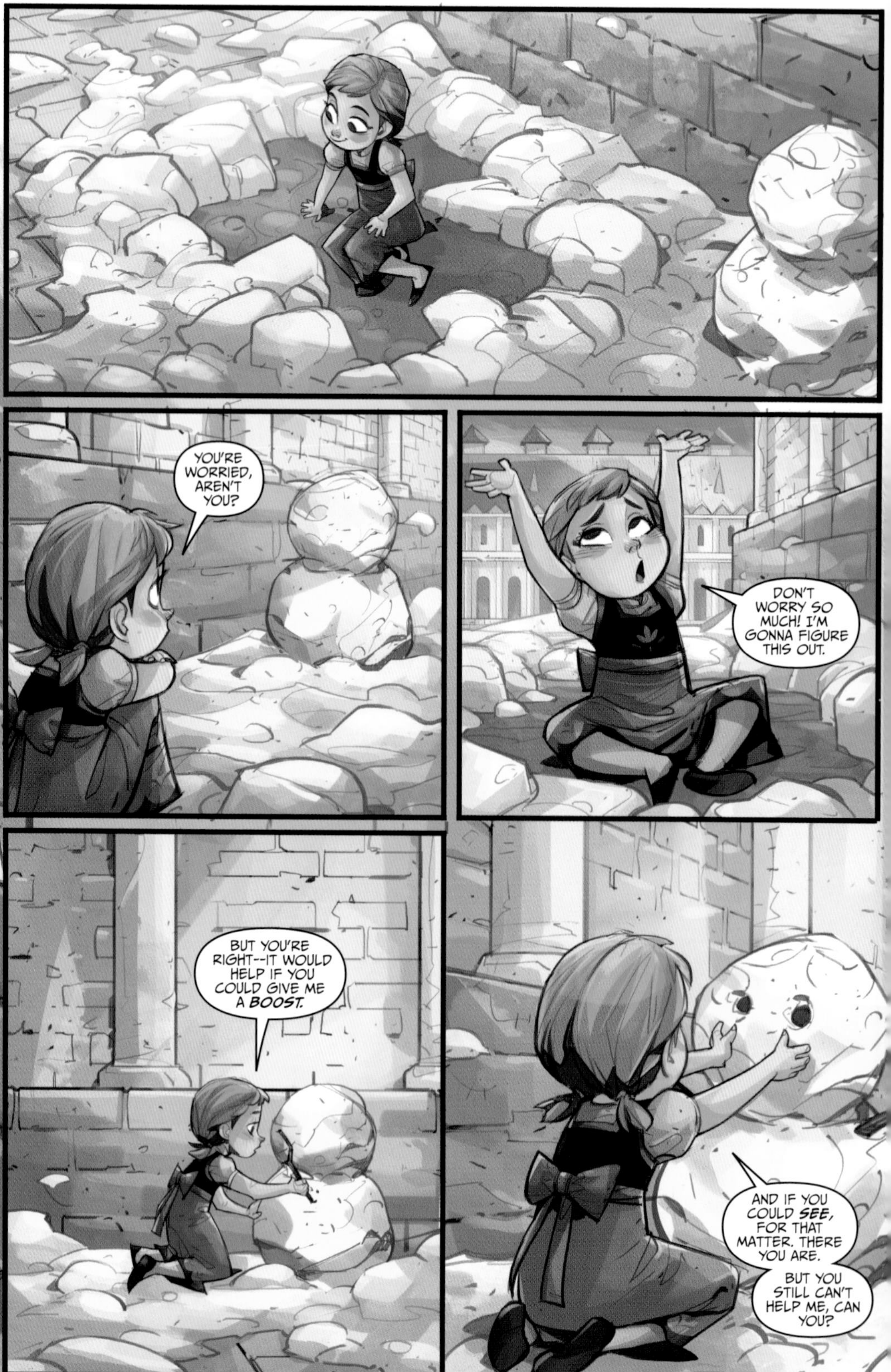
YOU'RE WORRIED, AREN'T YOU?
DON'T WORRY SO MUCH! I'M GONNA FIGURE THIS OUT.
BUT YOU'RE RIGHT--IT WOULD HELP IF YOU COULD GIVE ME A *BOOST.*
AND IF YOU COULD ***SEE,*** FOR THAT MATTER. THERE YOU ARE.
BUT YOU STILL CAN'T HELP ME, CAN YOU?

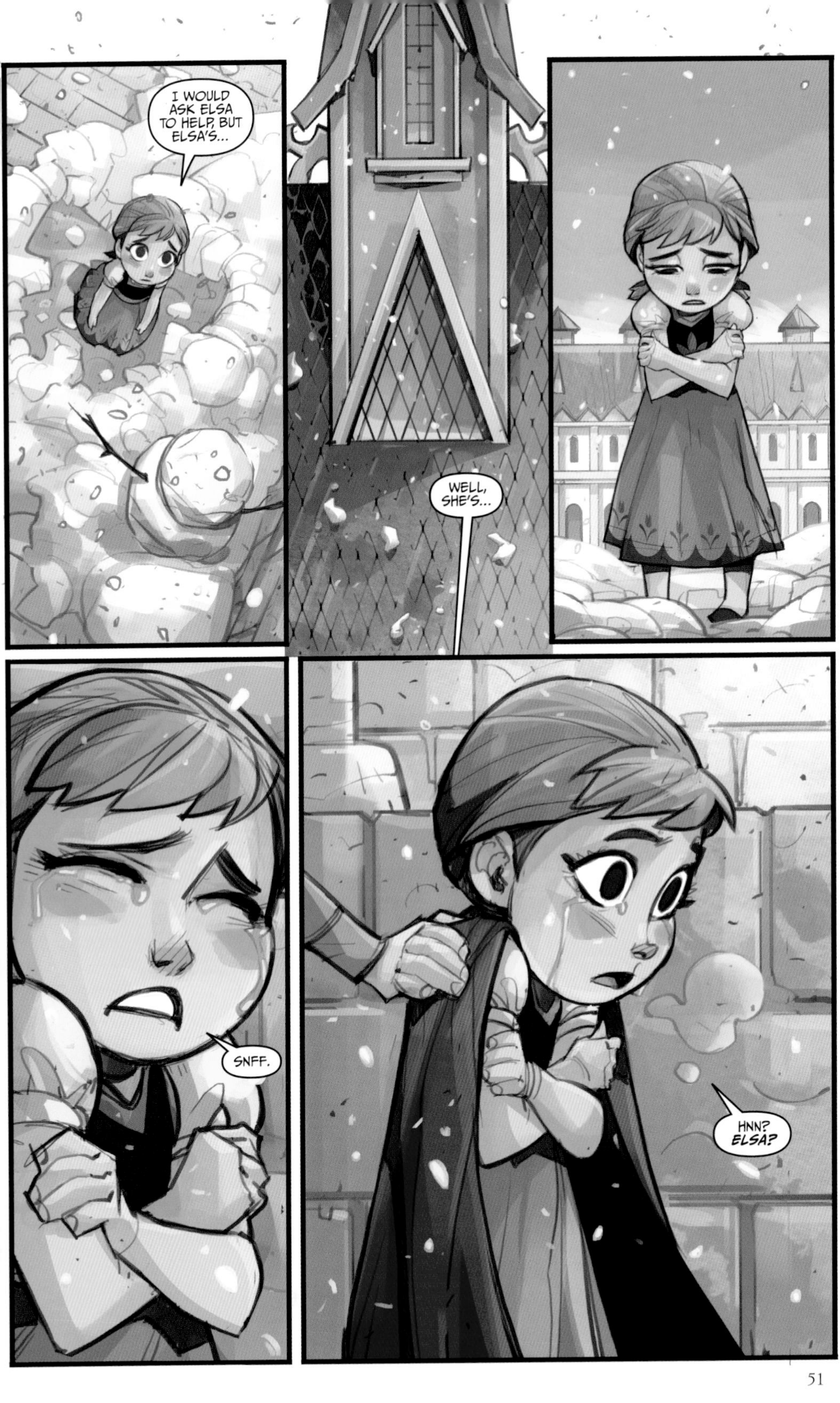
I WOULD ASK ELSA TO HELP, BUT ELSA'S...
WELL, SHE'S...
SNFF.
HNN? *ELSA?*

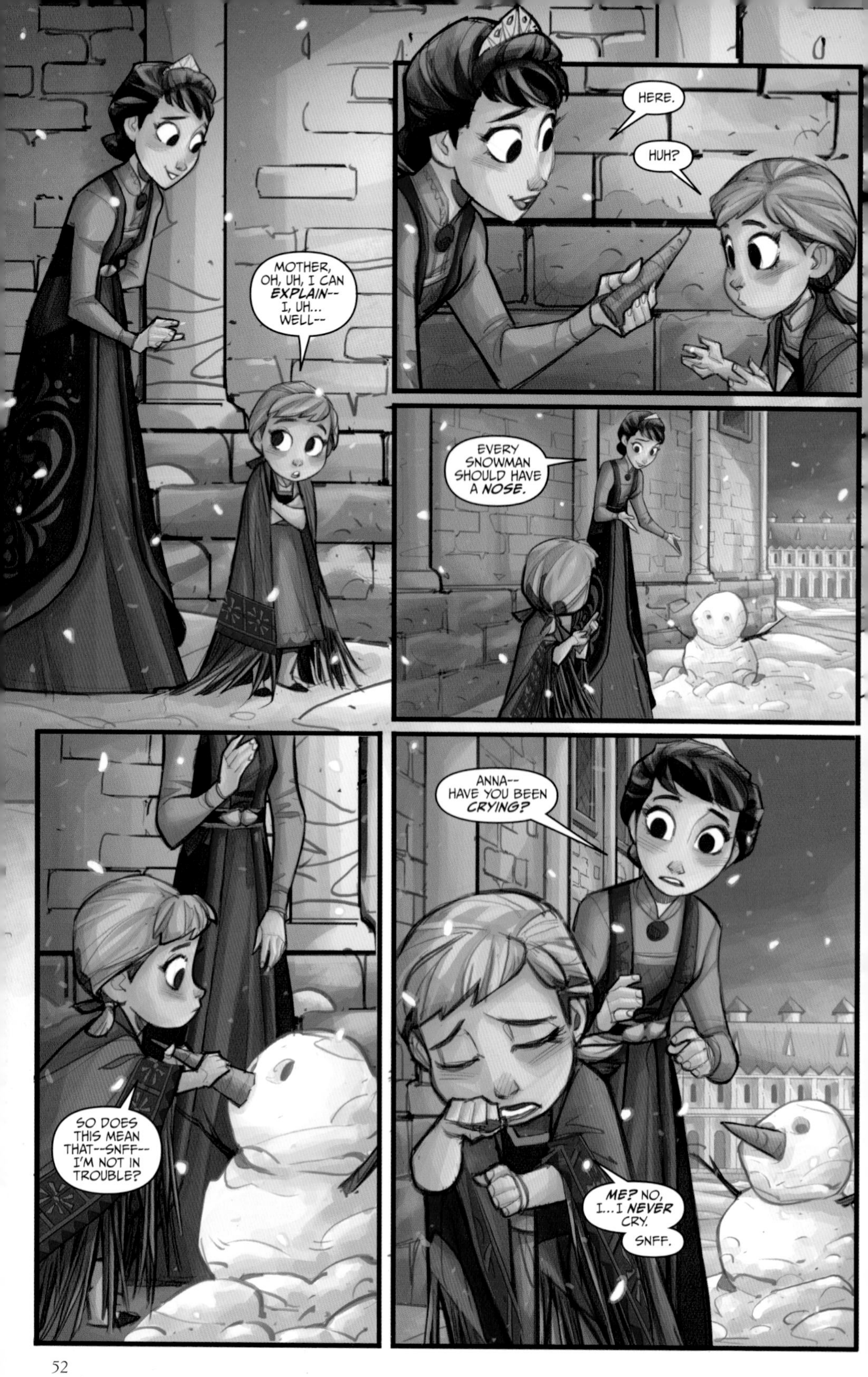

MOTHER, OH, UH, I CAN EXPLAIN-- I, UH... WELL--
HERE.
HUH?
EVERY SNOWMAN SHOULD HAVE A NOSE.
SO DOES THIS MEAN THAT--SNFF-- I'M NOT IN TROUBLE?
ANNA-- HAVE YOU BEEN CRYING?
ME? NO, I...I NEVER CRY.
SNFF.

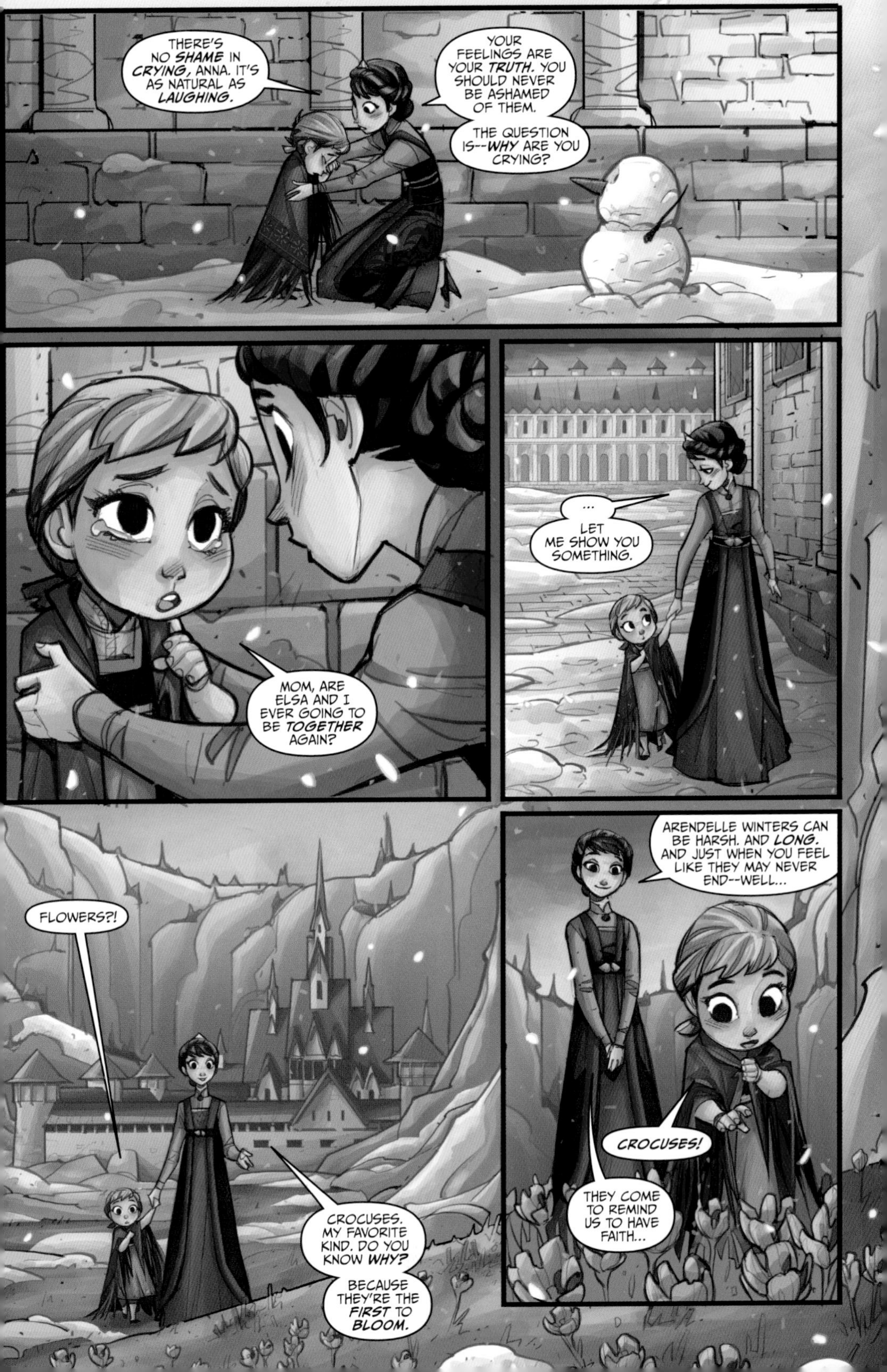
THERE'S NO SHAME IN CRYING, ANNA. IT'S AS NATURAL AS LAUGHING.
YOUR FEELINGS ARE YOUR TRUTH. YOU SHOULD NEVER BE ASHAMED OF THEM.
THE QUESTION IS--WHY ARE YOU CRYING?
MOM, ARE ELSA AND I EVER GOING TO BE TOGETHER AGAIN?
...
LET ME SHOW YOU SOMETHING.
FLOWERS?!
CROCUSES. MY FAVORITE KIND. DO YOU KNOW WHY?
BECAUSE THEY'RE THE FIRST TO BLOOM.
ARENDELLE WINTERS CAN BE HARSH. AND LONG. AND JUST WHEN YOU FEEL LIKE THEY MAY NEVER END--WELL...
CROCUSES!
THEY COME TO REMIND US TO HAVE FAITH...

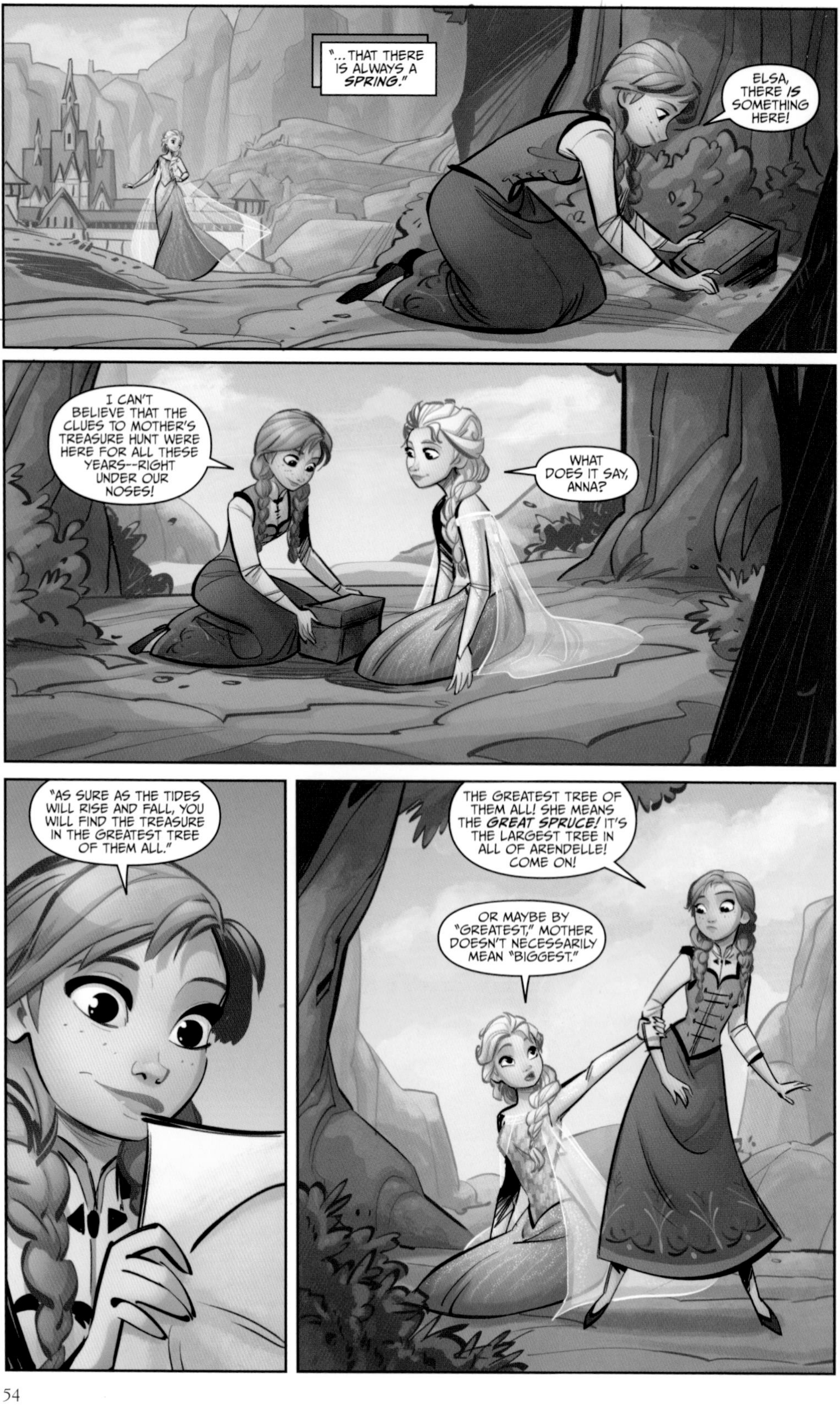
"...THAT THERE IS ALWAYS A *SPRING.*"
ELSA, THERE *IS* SOMETHING HERE!
I CAN'T BELIEVE THAT THE CLUES TO MOTHER'S TREASURE HUNT WERE HERE FOR ALL THESE YEARS--RIGHT UNDER OUR NOSES!
WHAT DOES IT SAY, ANNA?
"AS SURE AS THE TIDES WILL RISE AND FALL, YOU WILL FIND THE TREASURE IN THE GREATEST TREE OF THEM ALL."
THE GREATEST TREE OF THEM ALL! SHE MEANS THE *GREAT SPRUCE!* IT'S THE LARGEST TREE IN ALL OF ARENDELLE! COME ON!
OR MAYBE BY "GREATEST," MOTHER DOESN'T NECESSARILY MEAN "BIGGEST."

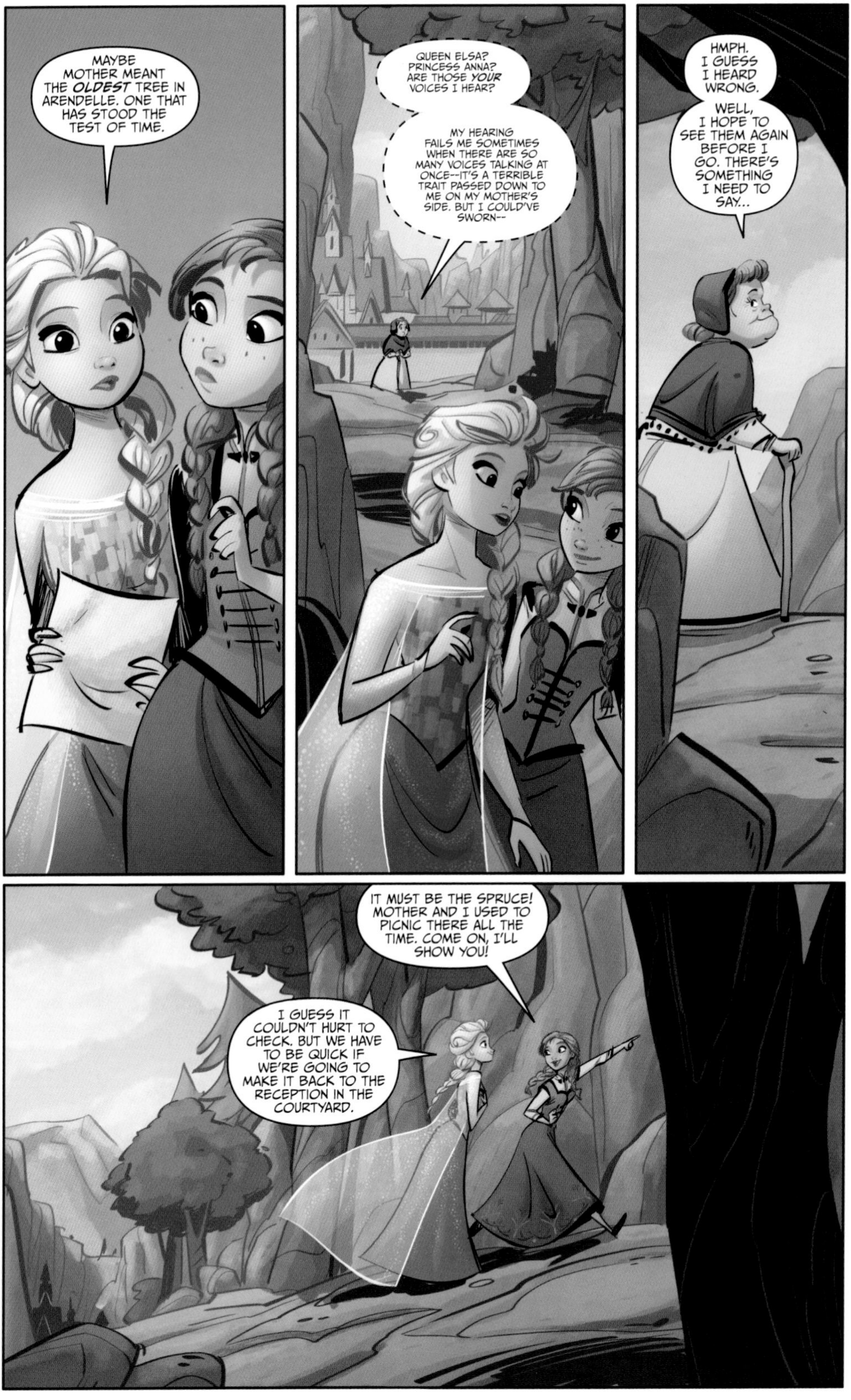
MAYBE MOTHER MEANT THE OLDEST TREE IN ARENDELLE. ONE THAT HAS STOOD THE TEST OF TIME.
QUEEN ELSA? PRINCESS ANNA? ARE THOSE YOUR VOICES I HEAR?
MY HEARING FAILS ME SOMETIMES WHEN THERE ARE SO MANY VOICES TALKING AT ONCE--IT'S A TERRIBLE TRAIT PASSED DOWN TO ME ON MY MOTHER'S SIDE. BUT I COULD'VE SWORN--
HMPH. I GUESS I HEARD WRONG.
WELL, I HOPE TO SEE THEM AGAIN BEFORE I GO. THERE'S SOMETHING I NEED TO SAY...
IT MUST BE THE SPRUCE! MOTHER AND I USED TO PICNIC THERE ALL THE TIME. COME ON, I'LL SHOW YOU!
I GUESS IT COULDN'T HURT TO CHECK. BUT WE HAVE TO BE QUICK IF WE'RE GOING TO MAKE IT BACK TO THE RECEPTION IN THE COURTYARD.

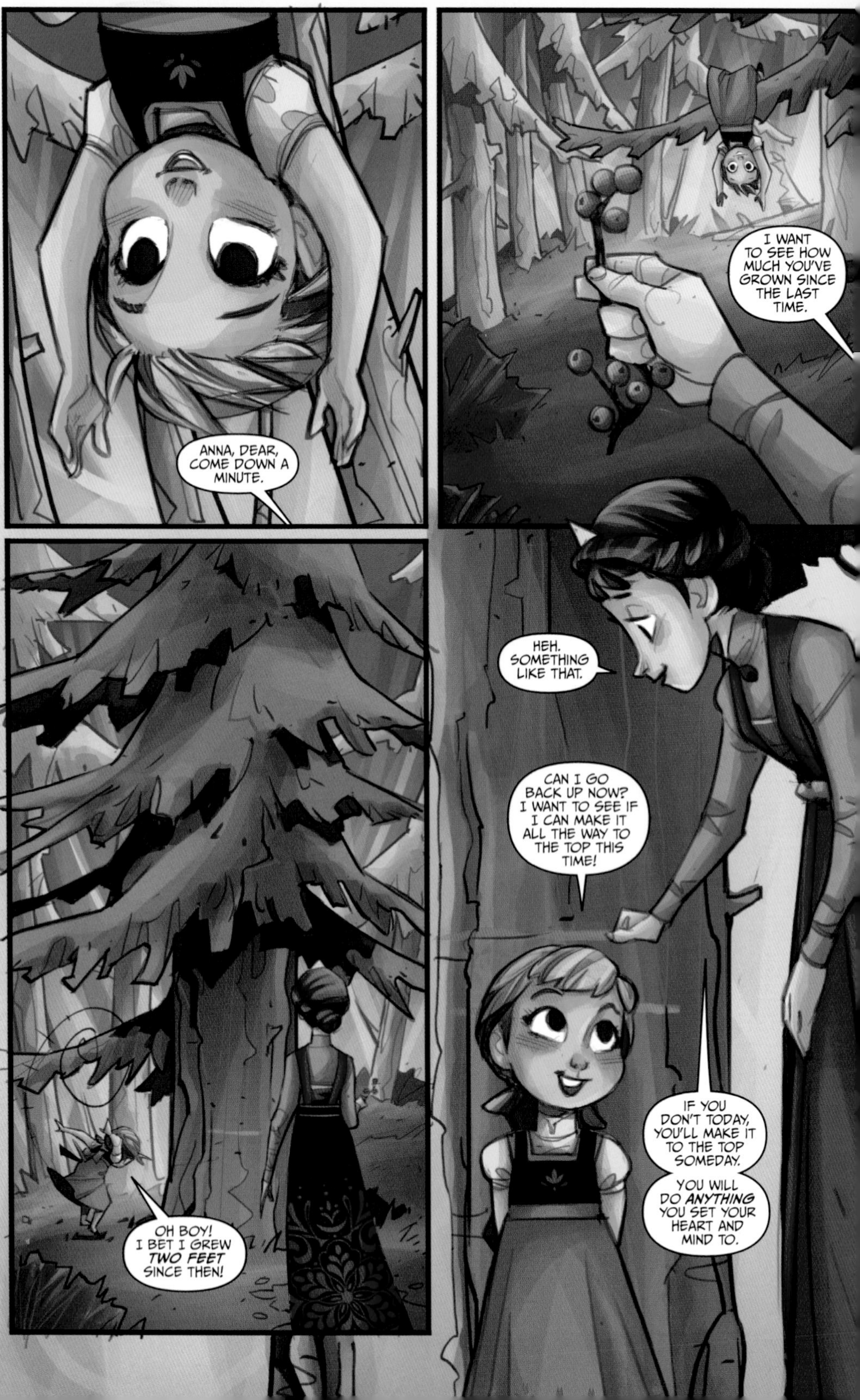
ANNA, DEAR, COME DOWN A MINUTE.
I WANT TO SEE HOW MUCH YOU'VE GROWN SINCE THE LAST TIME.
OH BOY! I BET I GREW **TWO FEET** SINCE THEN!
HEH. SOMETHING LIKE THAT.
CAN I GO BACK UP NOW? I WANT TO SEE IF I CAN MAKE IT ALL THE WAY TO THE TOP THIS TIME!
IF YOU DON'T TODAY, YOU'LL MAKE IT TO THE TOP SOMEDAY.
YOU WILL DO **ANYTHING** YOU SET YOUR HEART AND MIND TO.

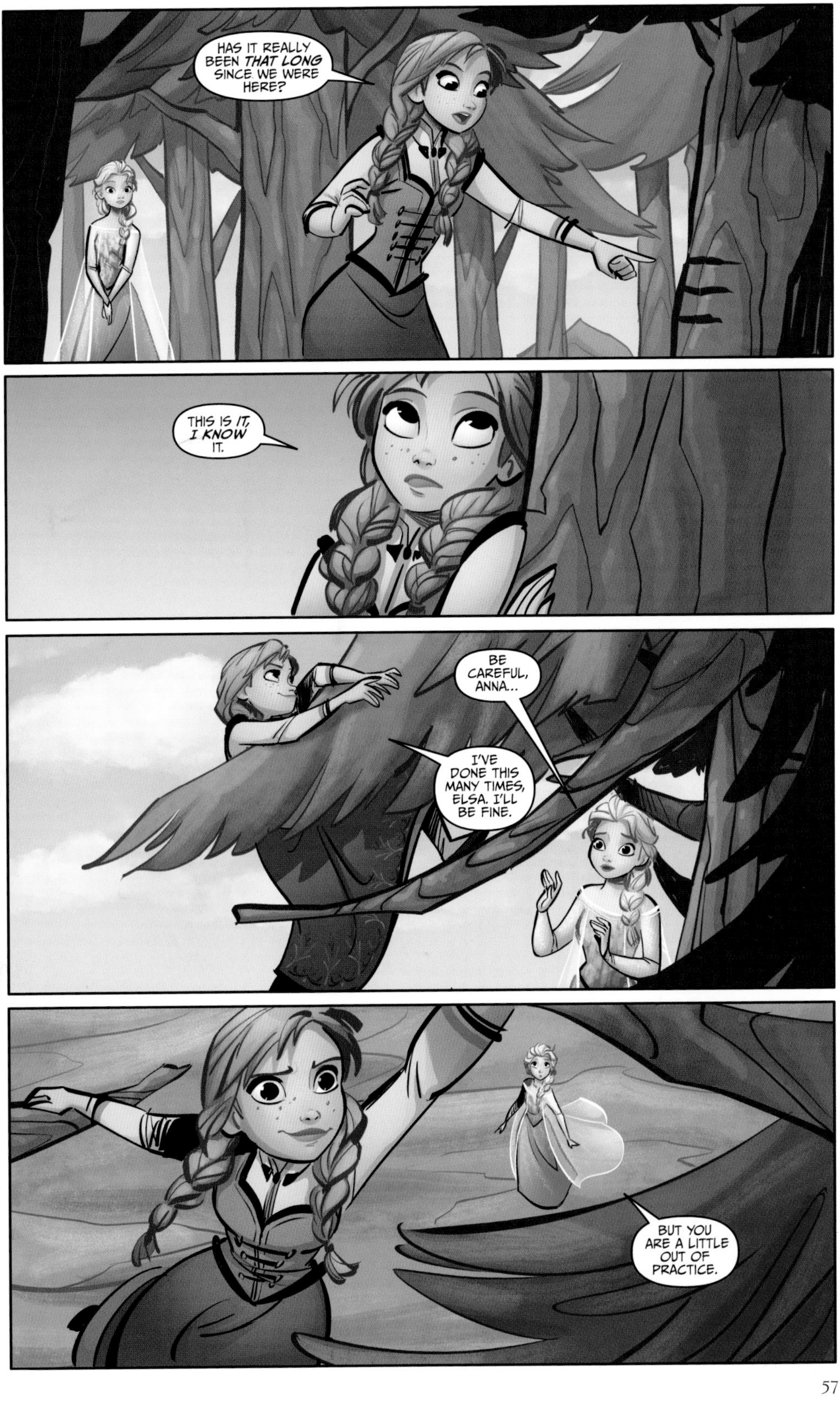
HAS IT REALLY BEEN *THAT LONG* SINCE WE WERE HERE?
THIS IS *IT*, *I KNOW* IT.
BE CAREFUL, ANNA...
I'VE DONE THIS MANY TIMES, ELSA. I'LL BE FINE.
BUT YOU ARE A LITTLE OUT OF PRACTICE.

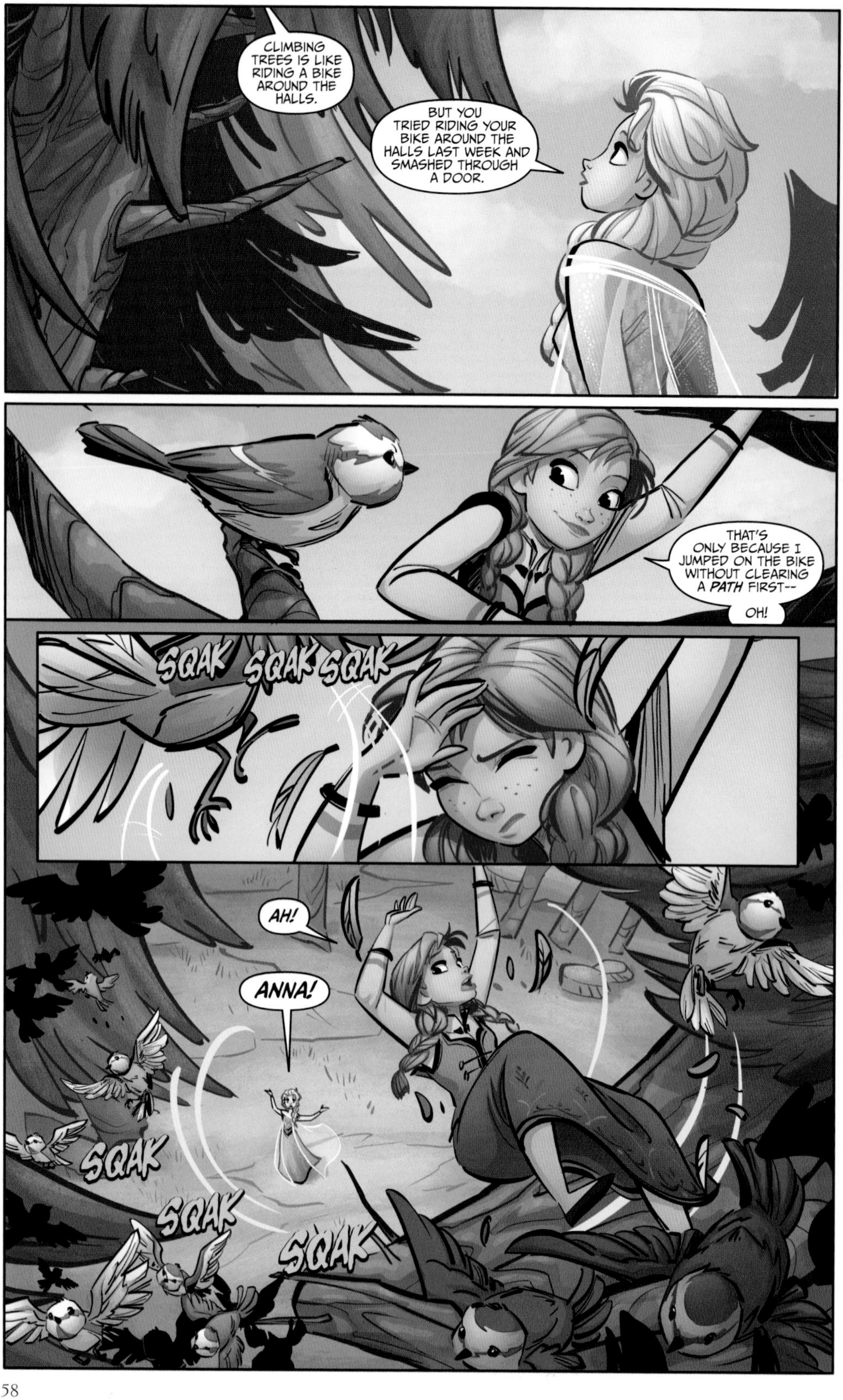
CLIMBING TREES IS LIKE RIDING A BIKE AROUND THE HALLS.
BUT YOU TRIED RIDING YOUR BIKE AROUND THE HALLS LAST WEEK AND SMASHED THROUGH A DOOR.
THAT'S ONLY BECAUSE I JUMPED ON THE BIKE WITHOUT CLEARING A *PATH* FIRST--
OH!
SQAK SQAK SQAK
AH!
ANNA!
SQAK
SQAK
SQAK

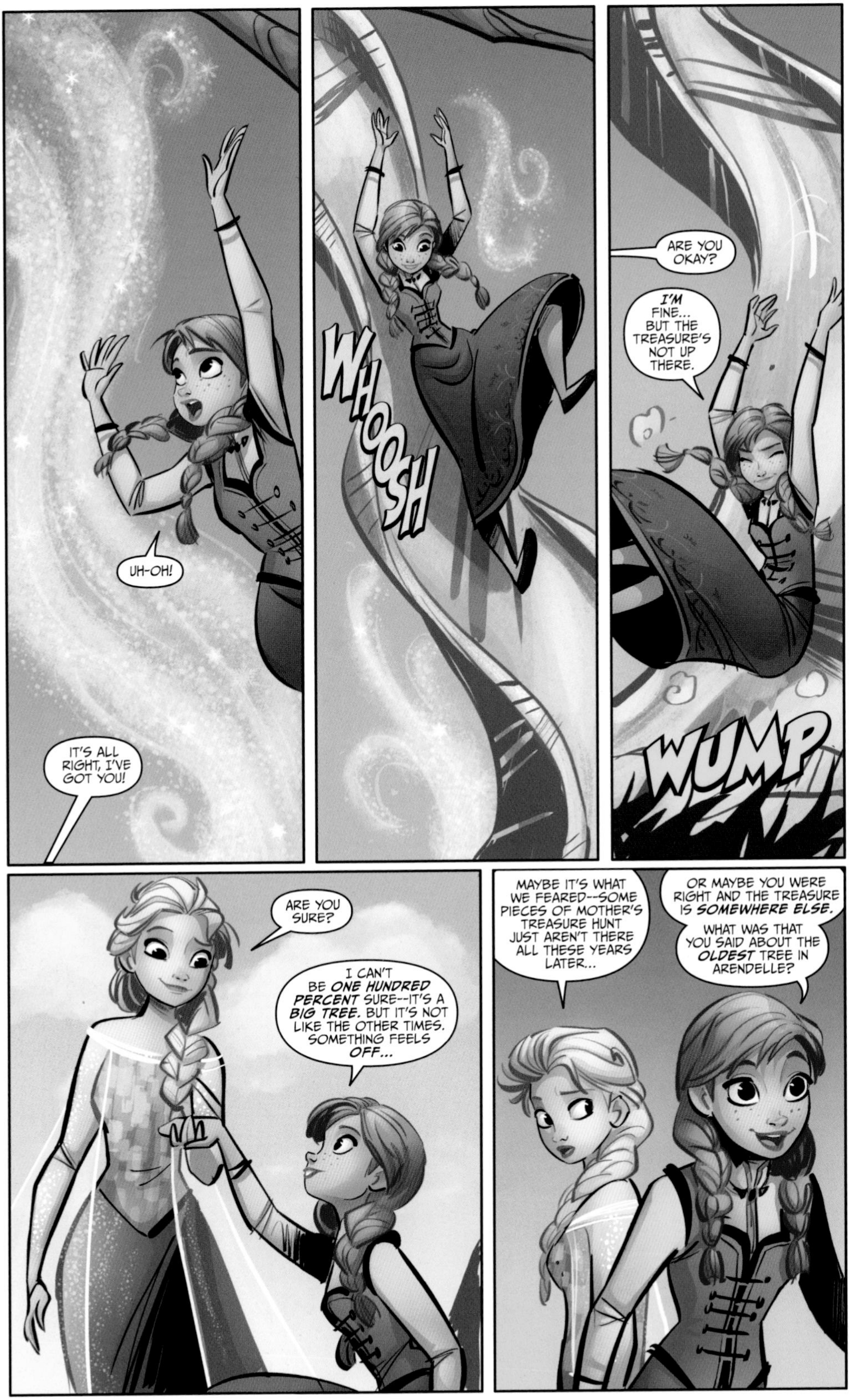
UH-OH!
IT'S ALL RIGHT, I'VE GOT YOU!
WHOOSH
ARE YOU OKAY?
I'M FINE... BUT THE TREASURE'S NOT UP THERE.
WUMP
ARE YOU SURE?
I CAN'T BE ONE HUNDRED PERCENT SURE--IT'S A BIG TREE. BUT IT'S NOT LIKE THE OTHER TIMES. SOMETHING FEELS OFF...
MAYBE IT'S WHAT WE FEARED--SOME PIECES OF MOTHER'S TREASURE HUNT JUST AREN'T THERE ALL THESE YEARS LATER...
OR MAYBE YOU WERE RIGHT AND THE TREASURE IS SOMEWHERE ELSE.
WHAT WAS THAT YOU SAID ABOUT THE OLDEST TREE IN ARENDELLE?

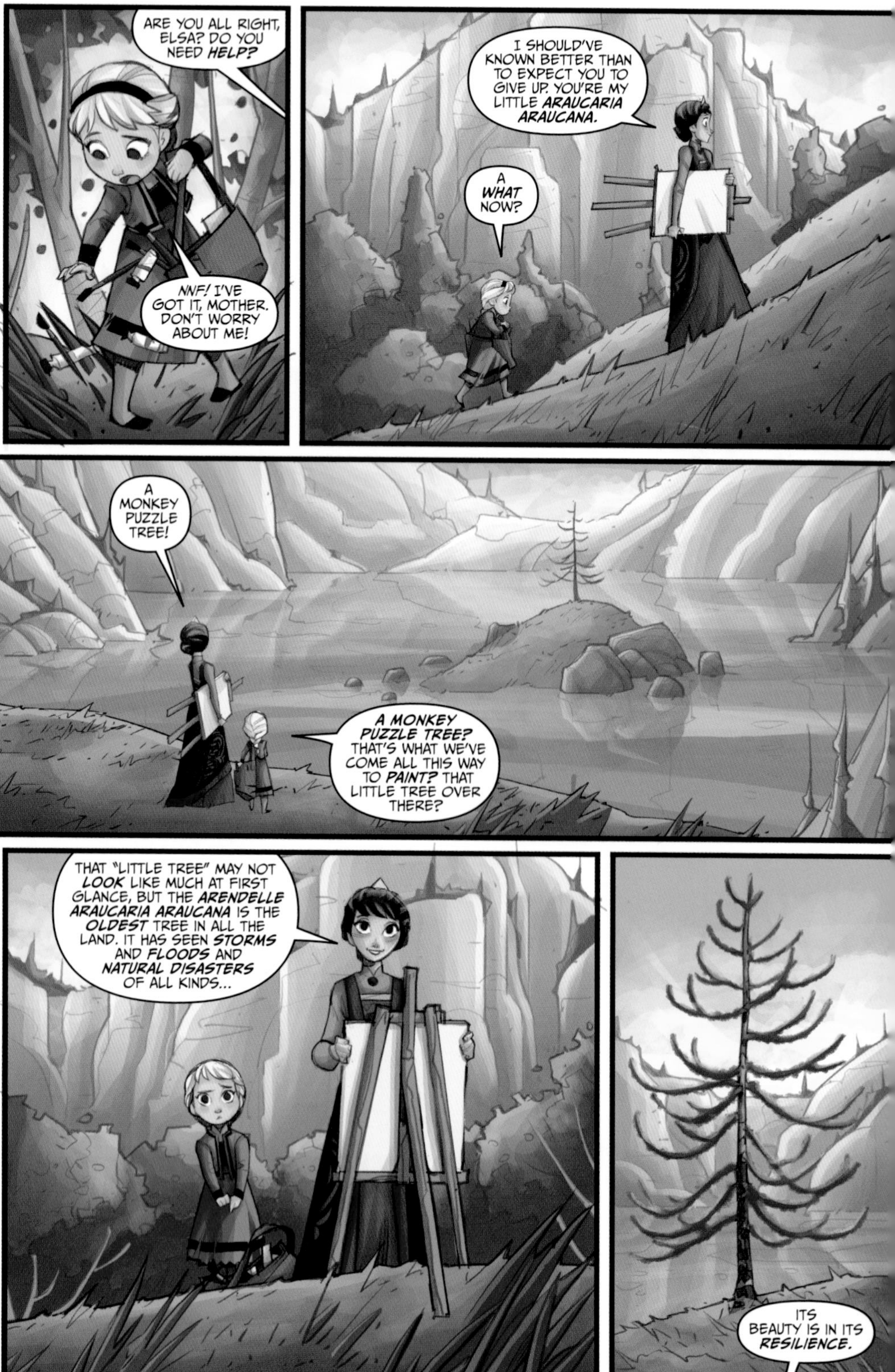

ARE YOU ALL RIGHT, ELSA? DO YOU NEED HELP?
NNF! I'VE GOT IT, MOTHER. DON'T WORRY ABOUT ME!
I SHOULD'VE KNOWN BETTER THAN TO EXPECT YOU TO GIVE UP. YOU'RE MY LITTLE ARAUCARIA ARAUCANA.
A WHAT NOW?
A MONKEY PUZZLE TREE!
A MONKEY PUZZLE TREE? THAT'S WHAT WE'VE COME ALL THIS WAY TO PAINT? THAT LITTLE TREE OVER THERE?
THAT "LITTLE TREE" MAY NOT LOOK LIKE MUCH AT FIRST GLANCE, BUT THE ARENDELLE ARAUCARIA ARAUCANA IS THE OLDEST TREE IN ALL THE LAND. IT HAS SEEN STORMS AND FLOODS AND NATURAL DISASTERS OF ALL KINDS...
ITS BEAUTY IS IN ITS RESILIENCE.

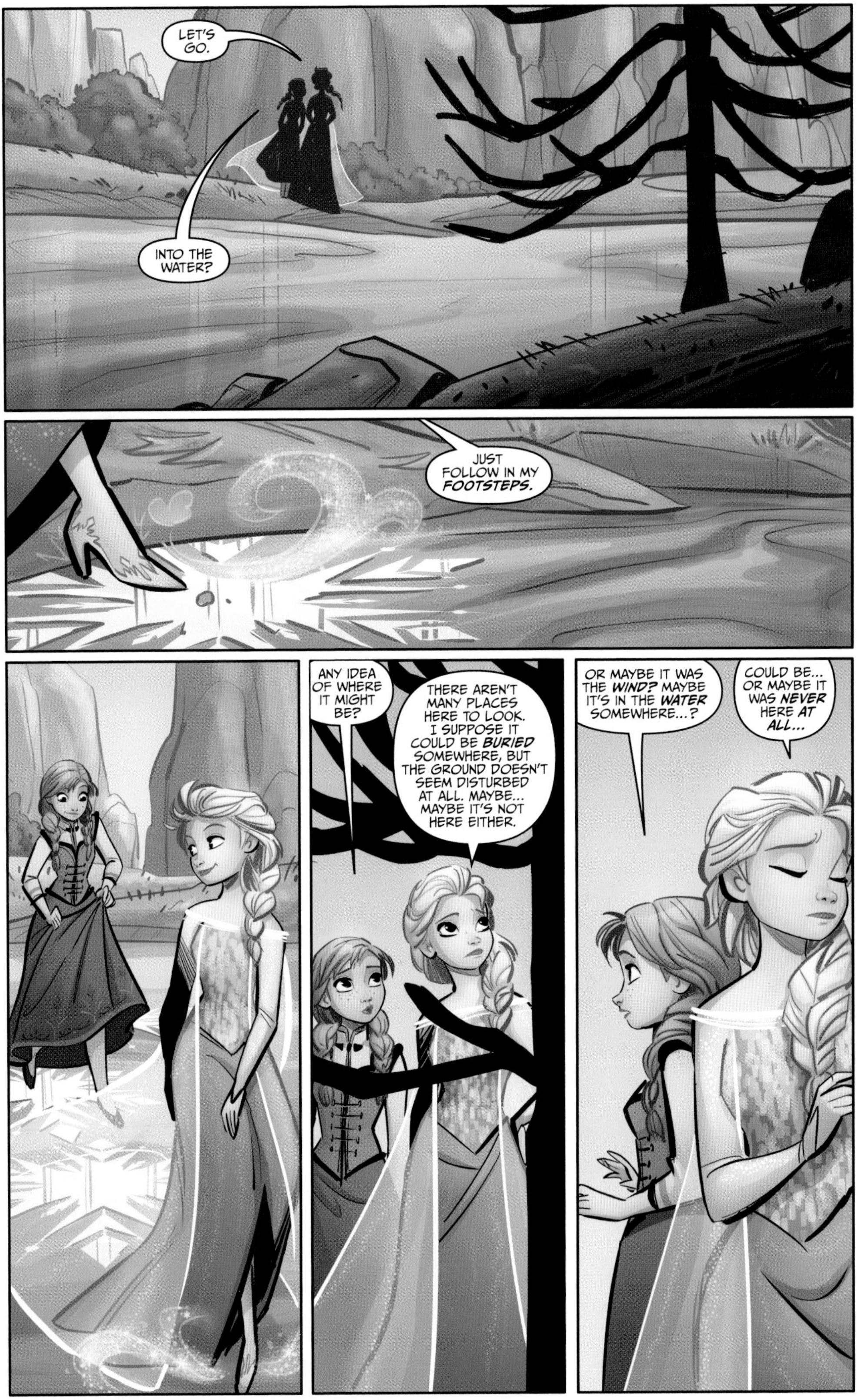
LET'S GO.
INTO THE WATER?
JUST FOLLOW IN MY FOOTSTEPS.
ANY IDEA OF WHERE IT MIGHT BE?
THERE AREN'T MANY PLACES HERE TO LOOK. I SUPPOSE IT COULD BE BURIED SOMEWHERE, BUT THE GROUND DOESN'T SEEM DISTURBED AT ALL. MAYBE... MAYBE IT'S NOT HERE EITHER.
OR MAYBE IT WAS THE WIND? MAYBE IT'S IN THE WATER SOMEWHERE...?
COULD BE... OR MAYBE IT WAS NEVER HERE AT ALL...

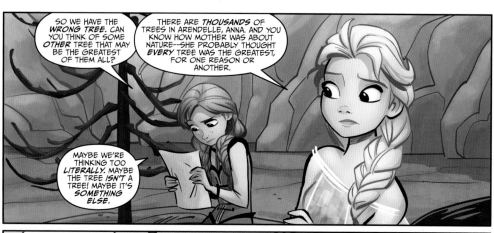

SO WE HAVE THE *WRONG TREE.* CAN YOU THINK OF SOME *OTHER* TREE THAT MAY BE THE GREATEST OF THEM ALL?

THERE ARE *THOUSANDS* OF TREES IN ARENDELLE, ANNA. AND YOU KNOW HOW MOTHER WAS ABOUT NATURE--SHE PROBABLY THOUGHT *EVERY* TREE WAS THE GREATEST, FOR ONE REASON OR ANOTHER.

MAYBE WE'RE THINKING TOO *LITERALLY.* MAYBE THE TREE *ISN'T* A TREE! MAYBE IT'S *SOMETHING ELSE.*

MAYBE "TREE" IS *CODE* FOR SOMETHING. OR MAYBE TREE IS A *PERSON!*

SOMEONE NAMED... *TREE?* YOU MAY BE *OVERTHINKING* IT, ANNA.

WE *HAVE* TO, ELSA. WE HAVE TO CONSIDER *ALL* POSSIBILITIES. WE HAVE TO FIND THE *TREASURE.*

WHAT WE HAVE TO DO IS GET BACK TO THE CASTLE. WE'VE BEEN GONE FOR SO LONG. IT'S ABOUT TIME WE JOINED THE RECEPTION.

WHEN MOTHER AND FATHER DISAPPEARED, IT WAS SCARY. BUT THE *WORST* PART WAS KNOWING WE'D NEVER *SEE* THEM OR *TALK* TO THEM AGAIN.

THE IDEA THAT THERE'S ONE LAST MESSAGE FROM MOTHER OUT THERE SOMEWHERE GAVE ME SO MUCH *HOPE.*

WE CAN STOP *FOR NOW* IF YOU WANT. BUT I WON'T GIVE UP.

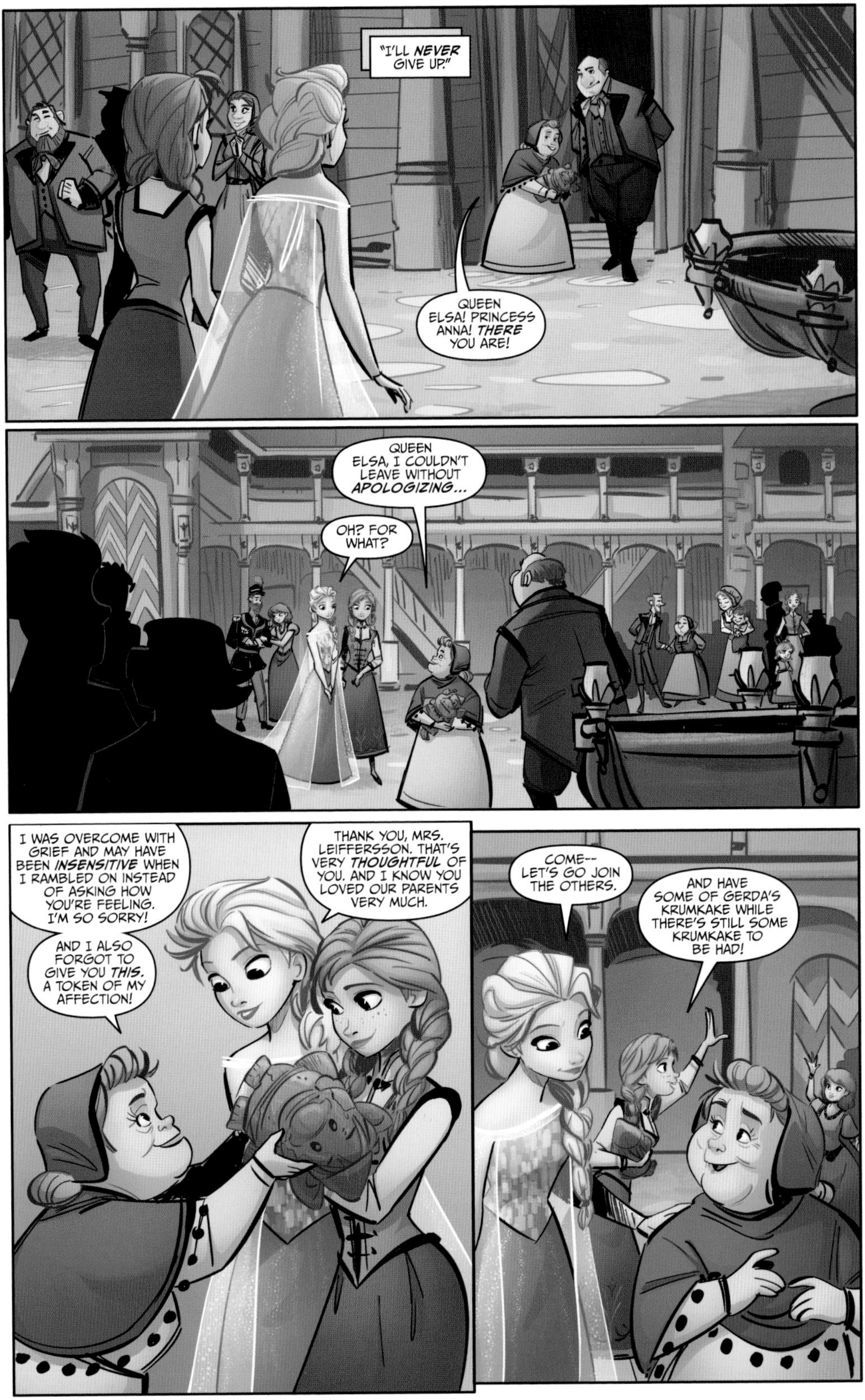
"I'LL NEVER GIVE UP."
QUEEN ELSA! PRINCESS ANNA! THERE YOU ARE!
QUEEN ELSA, I COULDN'T LEAVE WITHOUT APOLOGIZING...
OH? FOR WHAT?
I WAS OVERCOME WITH GRIEF AND MAY HAVE BEEN INSENSITIVE WHEN I RAMBLED ON INSTEAD OF ASKING HOW YOU'RE FEELING. I'M SO SORRY!
AND I ALSO FORGOT TO GIVE YOU THIS. A TOKEN OF MY AFFECTION!
THANK YOU, MRS. LEIFFERSSON. THAT'S VERY THOUGHTFUL OF YOU. AND I KNOW YOU LOVED OUR PARENTS VERY MUCH.
COME-- LET'S GO JOIN THE OTHERS.
AND HAVE SOME OF GERDA'S KRUMKAKE WHILE THERE'S STILL SOME KRUMKAKE TO BE HAD!

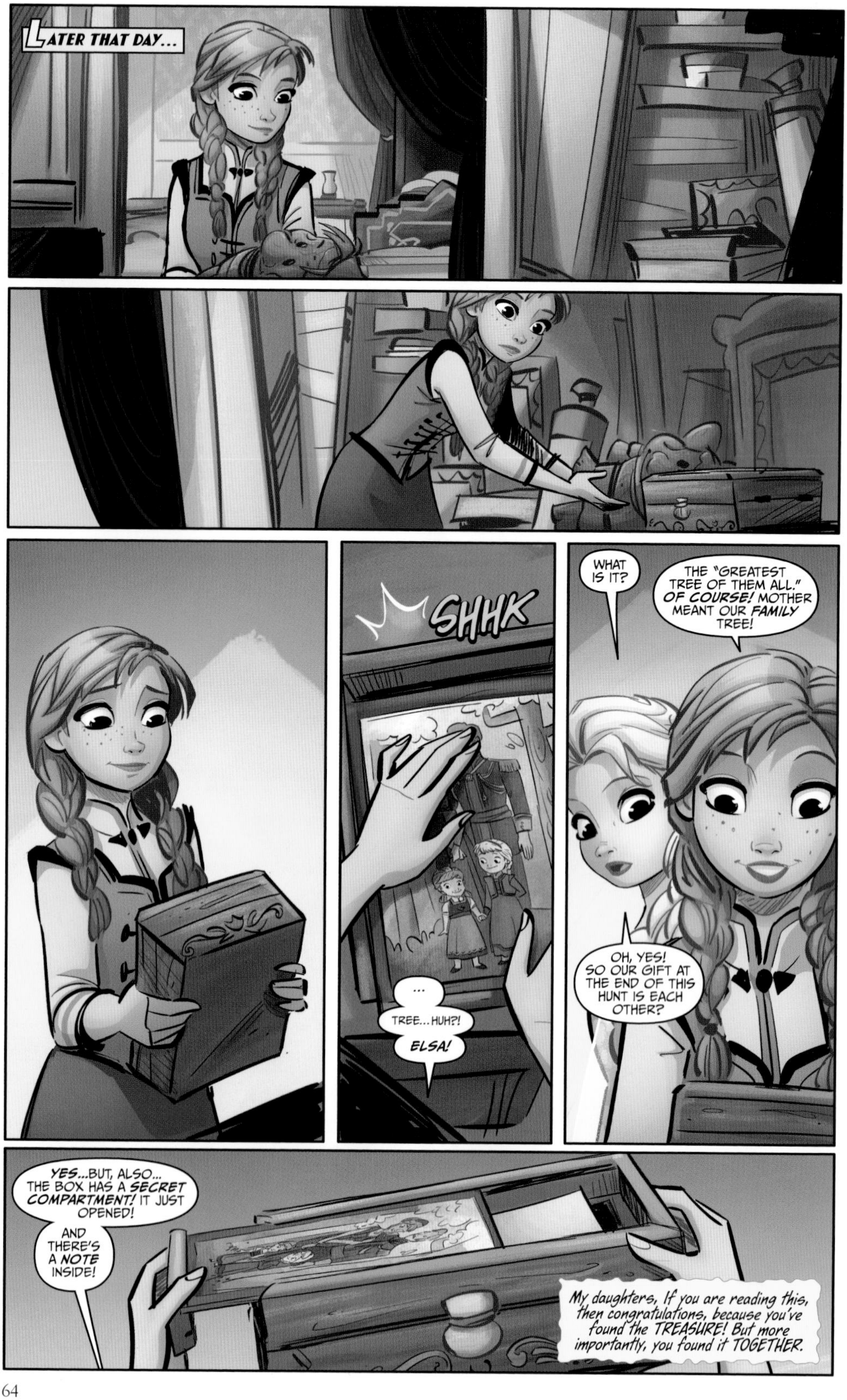

LATER THAT DAY...
SHHK
...
TREE... HUH?!
ELSA!
WHAT IS IT?
THE "GREATEST TREE OF THEM ALL." OF COURSE! MOTHER MEANT OUR FAMILY TREE!
OH, YES! SO OUR GIFT AT THE END OF THIS HUNT IS EACH OTHER?
YES...BUT, ALSO... THE BOX HAS A SECRET COMPARTMENT! IT JUST OPENED!
AND THERE'S A NOTE INSIDE!
My daughters, If you are reading this, then congratulations, because you've found the TREASURE! But more importantly, you found it TOGETHER.

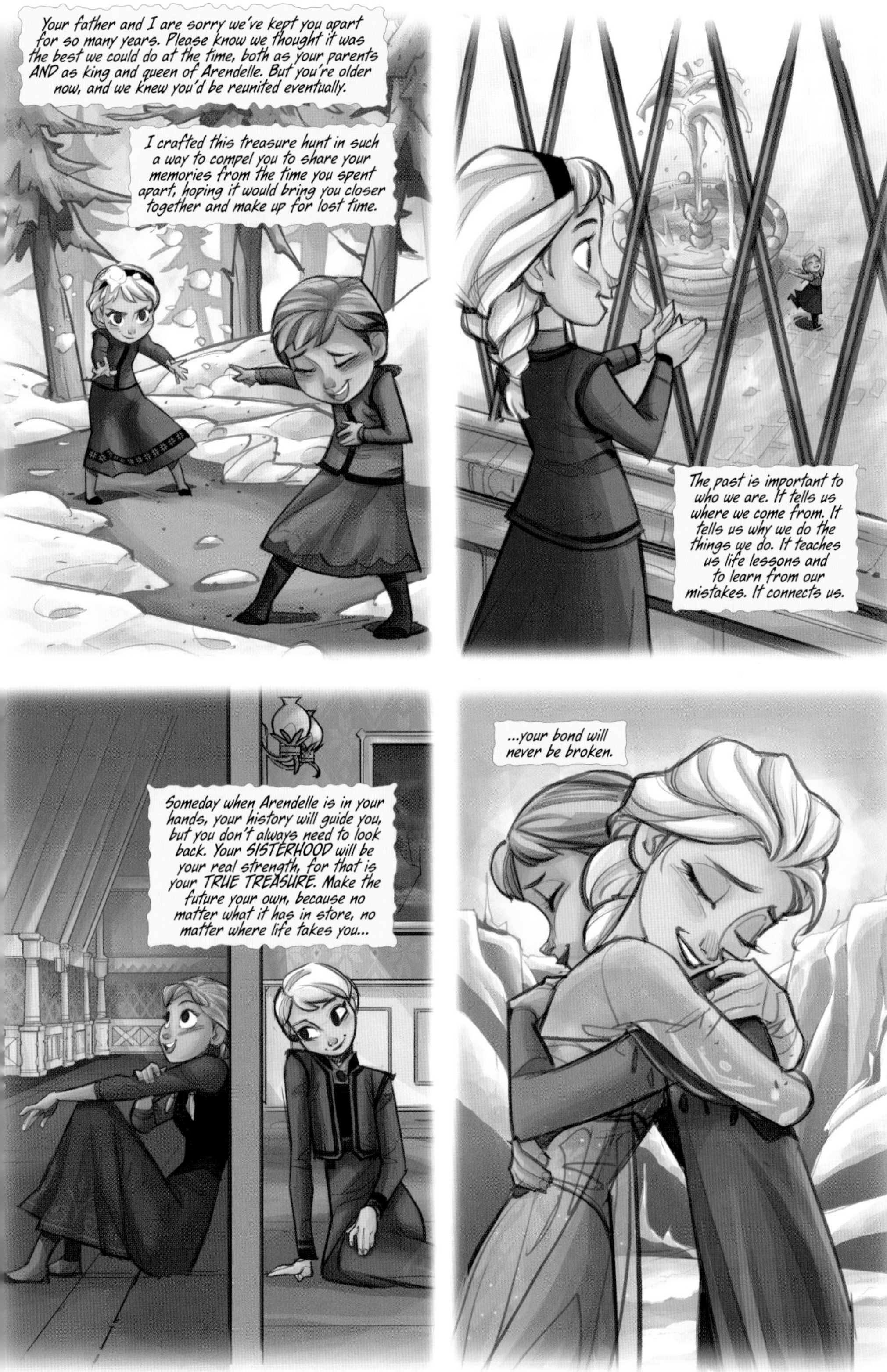
Your father and I are sorry we've kept you apart for so many years. Please know we thought it was the best we could do at the time, both as your parents AND as king and queen of Arendelle. But you're older now, and we knew you'd be reunited eventually.
I crafted this treasure hunt in such a way to compel you to share your memories from the time you spent apart, hoping it would bring you closer together and make up for lost time.
The past is important to who we are. It tells us where we come from. It tells us why we do the things we do. It teaches us life lessons and to learn from our mistakes. It connects us.
Someday when Arendelle is in your hands, your history will guide you, but you don't always need to look back. Your SISTERHOOD will be your real strength, for that is your TRUE TREASURE. Make the future your own, because no matter what it has in store, no matter where life takes you...
...your bond will never be broken.

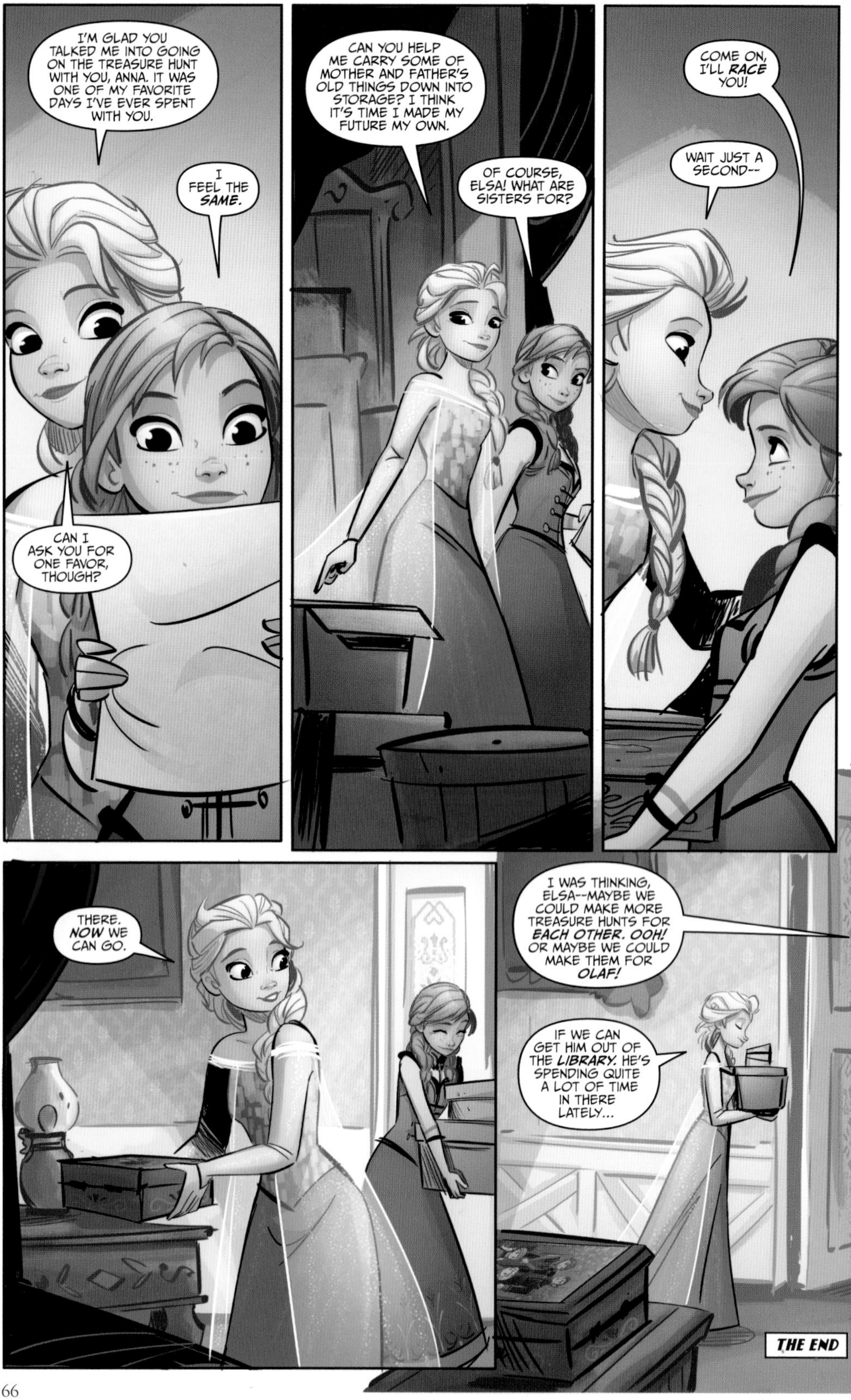
I'M GLAD YOU TALKED ME INTO GOING ON THE TREASURE HUNT WITH YOU, ANNA. IT WAS ONE OF MY FAVORITE DAYS I'VE EVER SPENT WITH YOU.
I FEEL THE *SAME.*
CAN I ASK YOU FOR ONE FAVOR, THOUGH?
CAN YOU HELP ME CARRY SOME OF MOTHER AND FATHER'S OLD THINGS DOWN INTO STORAGE? I THINK IT'S TIME I MADE MY FUTURE MY OWN.
OF COURSE, ELSA! WHAT ARE SISTERS FOR?
COME ON, I'LL *RACE* YOU!
WAIT JUST A SECOND--
THERE. *NOW* WE CAN GO.
I WAS THINKING, ELSA--MAYBE WE COULD MAKE MORE TREASURE HUNTS FOR *EACH OTHER. OOH!* OR MAYBE WE COULD MAKE THEM FOR *OLAF!*
IF WE CAN GET HIM OUT OF THE *LIBRARY.* HE'S SPENDING QUITE A LOT OF TIME IN THERE LATELY...
THE END